Puffin Books

krakatoa lighthouse

Suddenly there was a trench across the beach, about ten metres away from the fishermen, where before there had been nothing but flat sand. The fishermen moved quickly away as the trench heaved grey ash across the sand. They sprinted when it hurled black rocks at them.

Kerta didn't want to go to Krakatoa.

He knows that a dark spirit, Orang Aljeh, is there and he is terrified that he might wake it. But Kerta is there on the volcano, and the Ghost of Krakatoa has woken up.

Also by Allan Baillie

Adrift
Little Brother
Riverman
Eagle Island
Megan's Star
Mates
Hero
The China Coin
Little Monster
The Bad Guys
Magician
The Dream Catcher
Songman
Secrets of Walden Rising
The Last Shot
Wreck!
Saving Abbie
Treasure Hunters
The Excuse
Foggy
Imp
A Taste of Cockroach
Cat's Mountain

Picture Books
Drac and the Gremlin
The Boss
Rebel!
Old Magic
DragonQuest
Star Navigator
Archie the Good Bad Wolf
Castles

Non-fiction
Legends
Heroes

krakatoa lighthouse

Allan Baillie

Puffin Books

PUFFIN BOOKS

Published by the Penguin Group
Penguin Group (Australia)
250 Camberwell Road, Camberwell, Victoria 3124, Australia
(a division of Pearson Australia Group Pty Ltd)
Penguin Group (USA) Inc.
375 Hudson Street, New York, New York 10014, USA
Penguin Group (Canada)
90 Eglinton Avenue East, Suite 700, Toronto, Canada ON M4P 2Y3
(a division of Pearson Penguin Canada Inc.)
Penguin Books Ltd
80 Strand, London WC2R 0RL England
Penguin Ireland
25 St Stephen's Green, Dublin 2, Ireland
(a division of Penguin Books Ltd)
Penguin Books India Pvt Ltd
11 Community Centre, Panchsheel Park, New Delhi – 110 017, India
Penguin Group (NZ)
67 Apollo Drive, Rosedale, North Shore 0632, New Zealand
(a division of Pearson New Zealand Ltd)
Penguin Books (South Africa) (Pty) Ltd
24 Sturdee Avenue, Rosebank, Johannesburg 2196, South Africa

Penguin Books Ltd, Registered Offices: 80 Strand, London, WC2R 0RL, England

First published by Penguin Group (Australia), 2009

10 9 8 7 6 5 4 3 2 1

Text copyright © Allan Baillie 2009

Cover and text design by Megan Baker © Penguin Group (Australia)
Maps illustrated by Andrew Joyner
Cover photographs flickr.com – Richard Anderson (silhouette of boy);
flickr.com – Ricard Giner (storm clouds); Jupiter Images (palm trees)
Typeset in Stempel Garamond by Post Pre-Press Group, Brisbane, Queensland
Printed and bound in Australia by McPherson's Printing Group, Maryborough, Victoria

National Library of Australia
Cataloguing-in-Publication data:

Baillie, Allan, 1943-

Krakatoa Lighthouse / Allan Baillie.

ISBN 978 0 14 330359 6 (pbk.)

Krakatoa (Indonesia) – Fiction.

A823.3

puffin.com.au

contents

VERLATEN ISLAND

POLISH HAT ISLAND

LANG ISLAND

PERBOEWATAN

DANAN

RAKATA

KRAKATOA ISLAND

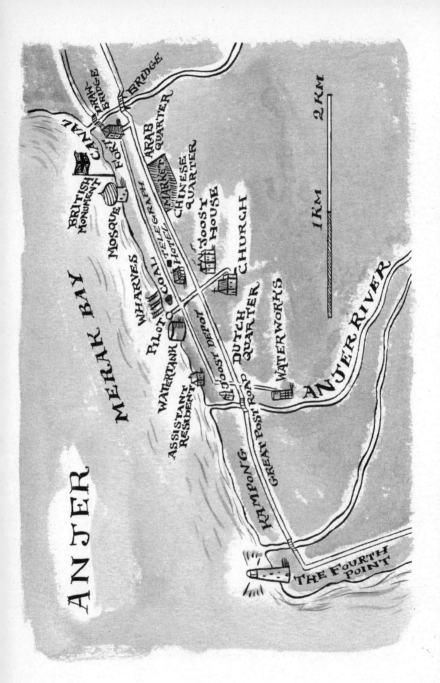

goliath

PA heard the sound first.

He had been ladling a wad of steaming rice onto his plate when he stopped and turned from the patterned mat. Kerta saw his father looking at the Dutch flag on the pole outside Jacob's bungalow.

Ma said when Pa was a fisherman the other fishermen believed that he could hear fish fins moving in the sea a kilometre away. Now he had heard something, and he was looking at the tricolour flag to measure air movement. The faded red top section of the flag was lifting, but the white middle was hardly stirring and the blue bottom was just clinging to the pole. The air was almost dead.

From the veranda of their hut Pa glanced at the open door of the white lighthouse and at the large corrugated water tank next to it, which Kerta's little sister, Dewi, called 'the baby lighthouse'. After a brief nod Pa looked towards the huts clustered around the lighthouse, but there was nothing happening. This was expected.

Apart from Pa, Ma, Dewi and Kerta the *kampong*, the tiny village, was deserted. Jacob had gone to the town – Anjer – with his twin boys, Dirck and Adam.

Jacob Schuit was Master Lighthouse Keeper of Fourth Point, but at the kampong everyone just called him Jacob. That was how he wanted it.

The other three keepers were not around: the Brothers were fishing and Carver was with Jacob's amah, Rara, in their kampong, so Jacob had left the lighthouse to Pa.

Pa liked that.

'Did you hear something?' Ma tilted her head.

Pa lifted two fingers, as if he was trying to pluck something from the air.

Kerta listened to the low waves outside the veranda, over the tinkling of Dewi's bamboo wind-chimes. 'There are some men over there . . .' he said quietly.

Dewi, shorter than a goat, sniffed and wrinkled her nose. 'There's a bad smell.'

'You don't know anything.' Kerta waved down his little sister.

'I do too!'

Pa nodded. 'There's soot in the air.'

'See!' Dewi pouted at Kerta.

'Where are the men, Kerta?' Pa said.

Kerta stabbed a finger at the beach. 'They seemed to be laughing.'

Pa looked at the men and a boy dancing on the sand, throwing up their arms and clapping at something in the water. The boy was capering around the men and shouting, but his words were lost in the waves. Pa tried to see what they were seeing but the water tank blocked his view. He put his fork and spoon on his clay plate and stepped down from the veranda and walked towards the tank. Then he trotted, ran and jerked to a stop.

Kerta began to hear faint, panicked calls from the sea.

Pa swung around. 'Kerta, get a knife!' Then he sprinted to the open door of the lighthouse.

Kerta barged into the hut and Ma's kitchen. Unlike the lighthouse or Jacob's bungalow, there were no windows in their hut, but there was enough sunlight filtering through the palm-mat walls to make it light inside. There were also walls in the hut where Pa and Ma slept, but Kerta and Dewi didn't have an outer wall where they slept.

In the kitchen, a large urn full of water and a large bowl sat on a broad piece of wood. Near this were tins, plates and several knives. Kerta hesitated. Which knife? The fish-gutting knife, oyster-opener, long knife, chopping . . . ?

He didn't know what Pa wanted the knife for.

Ma slid into the hut. From a cracked leather sheath hanging on the inner wall she took a long, wavy blade and thrust it into his hands. 'That will do.'

Kerta stared at the knife, its steel blade rippling. It was longer than a machete, with a slight hook on its dark hilt. He had not touched it before, except for the rare furtive nudge. 'Um . . .'

'Come on, hurry.'

Kerta ducked his head, gripped the old wooden hilt and ran from the hut, flashing the blade as he moved.

It's not my fault, he thought. I know this is a special thing, Pa. I know you took this *kris* from a Sulu pirate in a fight, but Ma took over. What could I do?

Maybe Pa was fighting pirates now. Kerta had never seen a pirate . . .

Kerta reached the water tank and saw Pa leaping from rock to rock with coils of rope on his shoulder. There was a small boat in the breaking waves, very close to the rocks.

No boat should be there – especially not that one!

Kerta hefted the *kris* higher and skipped down the sand to the rocks.

The waves were gentle today, but there was always a current there. Fishermen never sailed close to the lighthouse's rocks and this boat didn't even have a sail. Kerta recognised it as one of the two steam-launches in Anjer. The other one was kept on its private wharf at the Assistant Resident's huge house, but this one was owned by Lloyd's Agent Schuit, the richest man in Anjer. He called it *Goliath* and had it polished every Monday by his boy, Bas. Before Bas got the job, he and Kerta had hung around together like green coconuts.

Schuit wasn't on the boat this time. Instead it was a new arrival in Anjer, Tuan Joost, a Dutch merchant who owned the town's depot. Wearing a white cap, he was shouting from the bow at Pa. Another man, a fair-haired boy and Bas were poking at the stern with boathooks. The boy was Joost's son, but Kerta didn't know who the man was.

Pa reached the edge of the rocks, spread his feet and pitched one end of his rope at Joost, who fumbled but finally caught it, pulled it down and tied it to the wooden bollard at his feet. Pa scuttled across the rocks towards the soft sand of the beach, holding his end of the rope up high.

The men on the beach were growling at Pa in what seemed to be disappointment. The skinny boy with them threw a couple of pebbles in Pa's direction, but he was too far away and the pebbles fell short. The boy didn't come any closer but he looked angry. Kerta had never seen him before.

Still holding the rope, Pa splashed into the water and waded away from the rocks, towards the yellow water where the river met the sea.

Kerta stood on a sea-lapped rock, looked at *Goliath* ten metres away and felt the weight of Pa's *kris*. He thought, Pa can't use this out where he is. He wants *me* to use it.

Scratching his cheek with the blade, Kerta studied the rocking steamboat and noticed the stern dragging. The fair-headed Joost boy was staring at him, as if waiting for him to act.

Kerta pulled his shirt off, tossed it on a dry rock and jumped into the water.

Pa now had the rope across his back and was heaving against the dead weight of the boat's bow. The bow was beginning to turn from the rocks, but the boat was side-on to the waves. Pa was almost motionless in the water and the stern was slowly drifting.

Despite the name, *Goliath* was only 23-feet long, not even the size of an ocean-fishing boat. But it gleamed, from the bow's bollard to stern's flag. The seats, the small wheel and the boiler were protected by a high white canopy through which the boiler's shiny brass funnel thrust, and whispered black smoke into the breeze. All the woodwork glistened. Polished brass covered the rim of the hull and the name *Goliath* stood out in shiny bronze letters from the bow. Lloyd's Agent Schuit's boat was prouder than the Assistant Resident's launch. He would be shattered if he lost it today.

Joost was at the bow, clambering quickly under the canopy and grabbing the useless wheel as the two men and the boy battled on at the stern.

Kerta thought, There is something jamming the propeller. Pa knew that from the moment he saw *Goliath*. That was why he wanted the knife.

Kerta took the *kris* in his teeth and swam towards the boat. Pa turned his head to the crowd on the beach and began calling at them, but Kerta couldn't hear his words through the shouting on the boat. On the beach nobody was moving towards the launch, but Ma hitched her sarong and started to wade towards Pa.

Then on the stern of *Goliath* a man with glinting glasses pointed at Kerta.

Kerta thought, they're Dutch, they probably think I'm a pirate and going to eat them.

But the man with the glasses clapped his hands. 'Good, good! That's what we need!' He was speaking in English instead of Dutch but there was a funny burr in his accent. He pulled his boathook from the water and waved his arm around the stern.

Kerta thought, Where else would I go?

He swam alongside the boat through the chopping and splashing water. He saw the Joost boy leaning over the stern and slashing at the water with a machete while Bas jabbed with his boathook. Kerta took the *kris* from his mouth and slapped it on the water.

Hey, I can't go down there with you doing that.

Bas looked at Kerta and his eyes shifted. 'Kerta.'

'Bas.' Kerta nodded at him.

Bas glanced at the boathook in his hands. 'I can't get in the water . . .'

'I know. Don't worry, we'll fix it.' Kerta jack-knifed down. The steamboat propeller was caught like a crab, hopelessly tangled and quivering inside a long black net. Kerta swung the *kris* at the net, but the force of the movement was lost in the water. When the blade hit the rope Kerta's body drifted away from the propeller.

He clicked his teeth in annoyance, grabbed the net and sawed at a knot near the propeller. That worked. He could feel the serrated edges of the *kris* slicing into the fibre and then the rope separated. But there were many ropes tangled around the shaft and blades of the propeller. He quickly attacked a rope around one of the blades, but he was running out of air. He tried to finish the cut, but the ache in his lungs was too urgent and he kicked to the surface.

Kerta heaved in a long breath then realised that Tuan Joost was leaning from the stern and saying something to him. He shook his head to clear the water from his ears.

Joost pushed his bright red face closer to Kerta. 'I said, what does it look like down there, boy?'

Kerta looked at him. He had seen Joost often in Anjer and knew who he was, but of course Joost wouldn't know Kerta from a bunch of monkeys. 'There's a lot of fishing net tangled up.'

The Joost boy was looking at him in an odd way.

'Those lazy Anjer fishermen ought to be hanged,' Joost growled. 'How long will you be?'

Kerta saw that the launch was jolting slightly because its bow was crunching into the sand. Pa and Ma had been joined in the water by some Javanese men and the bow was now clear of the rocks, but *Goliath* was running out of space.

'I don't know.' Kerta shrugged. 'It's a lot of rope.'

Joost turned to Bas.

Bas shrivelled. 'I can't . . .'

'I can do it!' The fair boy ripped off his shirt, grabbed a machete and dived into the water.

'Jan!' Joost clutched at the air after him.

'The propeller is trying to turn but the rope stops it,' Kerta said, looking at the boy's splash.

Joost blinked at Kerta as if he couldn't understand him. But then his eyes shifted to his son's ripples. 'God.' He bolted to the engine under the brass funnel. He jerked the gear lever and wiped his mouth with the back of his hand.

Kerta dived and joined the fair-headed boy – Jan? – at the tangled net with some surprise. The boy was Dutch and Kerta didn't know any of the Dutch could swim, but he was hacking at the ropes like a Javanese fisherman. As he tapped Jan's shoulder, Kerta noted that the propeller was now motionless. When Jan stopped waving the machete around Kerta showed him how he had learned to cut the ropes. Jan nodded and went to the other side of the propeller to saw at another rope. Kerta was grinning as he attacked the rope he had left.

That was the first time any Dutch boy had followed him.

Soon Jan left for some air, but not before cutting through a rope. Kerta went through two and then yanked one from the propeller before going up.

When Kerta broke water Joost shouted, 'How much longer?'

Kerta gulped air and saw the stern rocking steadily towards the rocks. The man with glasses and Bas were using boathooks to push *Goliath* away from the rocks, but the waves were winning.

'Soon, soon,' he gasped, and dived.

Now the short seaweed was stroking the bottom of the rudder. Kerta immediately attacked a rope, but he was certain that it was too late. Those rocks on Jan's side were about to touch the hull and they would bang against the boat's planks until the water poured through . . .

Then Jan cut through a knot and Kerta felt his rope give way. He frowned at it, and pulled with both hands. The net came away from the propeller shaft; the blades turned and began to unravel the ropes. Jan saw what was happening, dropped his machete and seized the rope behind Kerta. They put their feet on the hull, heaved and the net rippled away from *Goliath*. They kicked to the surface.

'We got it, we got it!' Jan yelled in Dutch, and held up a handful of the net.

Joost nodded and waved him away. 'Move, Jan!' He hurried to the engine and pulled a lever. The water around the stern boiled.

Jan clapped his hands. 'Yes, yes!'

Kerta grabbed his shoulder. 'We have to go.' He pulled the net away from the boat.

The stern slowly swung away from the rocks. Joost shouted at Bas but he was already scuttling to the bow to throw Pa's rope off the bollard. For a brief moment the propeller churned the water, the bow rocked and then *Goliath* slid from the sand. The man in glasses shouted thanks at Pa and the others in the water.

Joost pointed his finger at Jan as he turned the wheel, but he seemed uncertain. The man in glasses moved to the side of the launch to pull Jan out of the water. Jan smiled at Kerta and began the swim to them, but Joost was watching the net coiling with the waves.

'No, no.' Joost waved his son away. 'It's too dangerous.'

Jan stopped swimming.

'You stay there, at Fourth Point.' Joost pointed at the lighthouse. 'I'll pick you up from there soon.'

He quickly swung the polished launch towards the open sea.

Jan stayed motionless in the water and stared at the shrinking boat.

the deal

'MAYBE he's worried about the propeller coming off,' Kerta said.

Jan shrugged. 'Why would a boy work on a boat if he can't swim?'

Kerta stopped. 'Bas? He can swim, or he did once. His father wants him on the boat to fix him up. But...' He shook his head.

The crowd on the beach that had refused to help save *Goliath* were shouting and gesturing at the rescuers. The other men who had joined Pa and Ma in the water were quickly wading away from them now. Pa and Ma turned from the beach and climbed the rocks to the lighthouse, a lonely couple. The shouters finally left them alone, but the skinny boy who had thrown pebbles at Pa was pointing at Kerta and then ran his finger across his throat.

'What's that about?' Jan said, paddling.

'I don't know.' Kerta shrugged and turned away from the skinny boy. He placed the *kris* on a rock and grabbed a handful of the net. He didn't want to know about it.

But Jan wouldn't let it go. 'These men who were shouting

11

and the angry boy . . . Was that because we're Dutch?'

'Maybe. Let's go in.' Kerta swam to the rocks, towing the net.

Jan dog-paddled awkwardly after him. 'They were cheering for us to drown.'

'You wouldn't drown, not here.' Kerta pulled himself up on a rock. 'Maybe get the launch a bit damaged.'

'But they were cheering.' Jan frowned. 'They were Javanese, weren't they?'

Kerta grabbed his hand and pulled him out of the water, frowning back. 'Well . . . this is Java.'

'You and your father helped save us but you're Javanese . . .'

'Pa is a lighthouse keeper.' Kerta started to pull the net over the rocks.

'Ah.'

But that wasn't all there was to it, Kerta thought. Just a part of it with Pa, but Kerta didn't know the rest.

Jan helped to pull the net, then he stopped. 'Oh, hell.' He was looking at the *kris*.

'What?'

'That machete I had. It's still out there.' Jan moved into the water.

Kerta caught him by the shoulder. 'I'll go. I know how to look.' He didn't wait for Jan to answer.

What am I doing? Kerta thought as he punched through the water. The Dutch boy said it. Pa's Javanese, I am Javanese and the Dutch have been sitting on us for centuries.

I should have been with the angry boy, not saving a Dutch steamboat. And what am I doing now, only being a lick-boy for a dumb Dutch boy . . .

He pushed the net sideways with the *kris* and saw the machete almost immediately. It was lying on the seaweed but the net had caught the handle, making it wobble in the water. Even Jan could have found it – blindfolded.

Kerta thought for a moment of leaving it there, but instead he plucked it from the net and kicked towards the rock.

'You were quick.' Jan's face showed his relief as he took the machete.

'It was easy.'

'If I lost that, Papa wouldn't forget it for a long time.'

Kerta glanced at the machete. 'It's only an old one.'

Jan shrugged. 'He's like that.'

'Oh.' Kerta saw Pa walking past the water tank, picked up the *kris* and hurriedly wiped it against his shirt. He wrapped the *kris* with his shirt and skipped over the rocks to reach Pa.

Pa stopped by the lighthouse door and waited.

Kerta passed the *kris* to Pa as if he was presenting a sword in its scabbard. 'It's not damaged, Pa, you can see. Ma gave it . . .' He saw a line of annoyance on Pa's face and left the words hanging.

Pa whipped Kerta's shirt from the *kris* and nodded. 'It's fine. It's not a statue; it can be something to use.' He passed it back with the shirt. 'I must go to work; take it and the Dutch boy to the hut. Ma will take care of everything.'

Kerta nodded and looked at Jan who was pulling the net over the rocks.

'Hey.' Pa stopped at the open door of the lighthouse and pointed at Kerta. 'That was a good job. Both of you.' He disappeared.

Kerta grinned and looked back to make sure that Jan had heard it, but he was staring at the top of the soaring lighthouse.

'You live there?' Jan said in awe.

'Well . . .' Kerta came back to help to pull the net.

'That's got to be great. When the waves crash against the wall in a big storm it must be like being in a fighting castle. I'd love to stay there.'

'A castle?' Kerta frowned at the lighthouse. He could remember how excited he was when Pa took him to the lighthouse for the first time two years ago. Then he'd thought it was a great warship ploughing through the worst of seas, or a dragon with its terrible glaring eye hunting ships in the dark. And Dewi had thought it was a magic tree. For sure, it was a cave full of demons, but a castle? That was for the Dutch in their fortresses in Anjer and Batavia. But . . .

He tilted his head, and looked again at the lighthouse. From the round brick base to its bronze weather vane the lighthouse was over forty metres tall, maybe higher than any tree in Java. A few times he had run through that red door, past the ropes, the kerosene lights, up the stone steps to the stores, swung up the trapdoor, and then clanged up the iron steps past the barrels of oil, past the bags of rice and tea, up, up, past the kerosene and tools, past the machinery of the light, past the balcony to the glass room. It was a long, hard race.

The red door looked like a mousehole in the granite. The narrow windows marched up the white tower to the iron balcony. Every night there was a fire up there to blast the night.

Well, it *could* be a castle.

'It's all right, I guess.' Kerta said.

'Do you want to swap?'

'*Goliath*?'

'No, Papa doesn't own *Goliath*, he only borrowed it to take a friend to an island. I meant our house – l have to live in a dull house in Anjer. It's on the same street as the church.'

'Near the cemetery?'

'Next to it, but it doesn't even have a single ghost.'

'Ah, they are there all right. Spirits are everywhere.'

Jan snorted. 'I didn't see anything.'

'Because you are white. The whites can't see anything.'

'Oh,' Jan said flatly.

'Never mind, come over to my place and get the salt off.' Kerta dumped the net near the water tank.

Jan started moving towards the lighthouse.

'Ah, no we don't live in there, we just work there.' Kerta led him towards the cluster of buildings.

'You live in that bungalow with the flag? That is almost as good as living in the lighthouse. You could jump from that veranda into the sea . . .'

15

'No, that's Jacob's house.' Kerta glanced at the house as he walked past.

The bungalow was propped on high rocks, catching all the sea breezes and a magnificent view of Sunda Strait. It had the same palm thatch on its roof as the huts around it, but that was almost the only similarity. The bungalow was as big as two ordinary huts and the walls were planks of wood instead of palm-mat. Kerta had been in Jacob's house many times and had seen walls everywhere, tables, chairs and soft beds and even a small glass window.

'That's mine.' Kerta pointed at the stilted hut. Apart from one slight alteration it was the same as the other three huts. The one difference was its veranda. The other huts had a wall of palm-mat and palm thatch protecting an outside deck living area from the sun and rain, but Pa wanted to feel the wind and taste the sea salt so his hut had an exposed veranda. Something to do with him being a fisherman once.

'Oh,' said Jan.

Dewi was sitting on the steps and folding her arms. 'You are very slow.'

Ma came out of the hut and smiled at Jan. 'Are you all right?'

'Oh, yes. Papa is going to pick me up.'

'Well, we better clean you up, first.' At the door Ma gave Jan a towel plus a shirt and shorts from Kerta. 'Do you know how to use a *mandi*?'

'Oh yes. We've got one in our house.' Jan followed Kerta across the kitchen to a wooden door. They stepped into a tiny room with green tiles, a big urn full of rain water and a coconut scoop beside it. Earlier in the day Kerta had used a clay pot to fill the urn with water from the tank.

They squirmed out of their clothes and Kerta threw scoops at Jan, who shrieked and retaliated with handfuls. When they stopped they were panting at each other and grinning.

'Now would you like to see my lighthouse?' Kerta said.

'All the way to the top?'

'If you're fit enough.'

Jan snorted.

Dewi was waiting for Kerta with a towel and her hand clapped across her eyes. 'You are very noisy.'

'You are a flea on a monkey.'

'Ma said there's a lot of people looking at the net. I don't know why. It's only a net.'

'Ah . . .' Kerta threw on shorts and joined Ma on the veranda.

There was a great crowd around the net. Jacob was leaning on his polished walking stick and talking with a short man wearing a tilted grey hat who was prodding the net. Jacob's twins, Adam and Dirck, were pushing at each other until their amah, Rara, clipped Dirck's ear.

No one knew what had happened to Jacob's wife apart from Jacob, and he didn't want to talk about it, but eighteen-year-old Rara had become the twins' mother and the empress of Jacob's bungalow. She was by the net because Carver had brought her there and he was examining it.

Kerta was frowning. 'Who's the man with the hat?'

17

Kerta watched little Dirck wandering around holding his hand over his ear with a shocked face.

'He was one of the shouters,' Ma said. 'But then he came out to help.'

'Why did they shout?' Kerta said with a furtive glance at Ma.

'There's nothing there.' Ma tapped Dewi's hanging bamboo. 'Like wind-chimes. They wanted to see any Dutch boat hit the rocks. But I don't think they wanted to see anyone hurt.'

'But why? They weren't doing anything.'

Ma laughed lightly. 'I don't really know. A bit of jealousy and of course the Dutch have always treated us like we're clever monkeys. But maybe it was like a cockfight. They wanted to bet against the Dutch – *any* Dutch – facing anything. Wind, tide, current . . .'

Kerta nodded. He had been right about the shouting. He should have been on the beach with the angry kid, except . . . . 'But after Pa shouted back, some of them joined us to save the Dutch boat.'

'See, it was a little thing.'

'What did Pa shout to them?' He watched Dirck fall over the net, but Jacob ignored him.

'He said this was different. Wasn't Dutch about the Dutch any more – it was only a boat and the sea. And that was something the fishermen understood.

'You better see what the man and the others want. Do you want help?'

18

Kerta looked at his mother, and shook his head. Pa would expect him to handle it. He slipped into sandals and padded across to the group. Dirck was pouting and still holding his ear as he pulled Jacob's trousers. Adam was grinning.

'She hit me!' Dirck said, pointing at Rara.

'Good, go away.' Jacob nodded to Rara and she pushed the twins towards the bungalow. When he saw Kerta he smiled. 'Dungu was telling me that you saved *Goliath*.'

Kerta recognised the man in the grey hat as one of the few men who had helped Pa with the steamboat rescue. 'Hi.' Kerta shook his head. 'Pa told me what to do.'

'Where is he?'

'He's up the top of the lighthouse.'

'Of course he is. I must go up . . .' Jacob looked over Kerta's shoulder. 'Jan?'

Kerta looked back and saw Jan walking down the steps wearing Kerta's ragged black shorts and green batik shirt. He looked funny.

'So you picked up this net, hey?' Carver smiled slyly.

'Yes.' Kerta turned. He had forgotten Carver's real name. Nobody used it. He whittled all the time so he was Carver.

'Maybe I can make something for you for it.' Carver's eyes were watching Dungu, seeing the disappointment in his face.

But then Jacob swung his stick and pointed at Carver. 'You are a lighthouse keeper and that's enough. Leave nets to the fishermen.'

Carver started to protest, but then he read Jacob's face, shrugged and moved away.

Jacob continued talking with Jan, leaving Kerta and Dungu alone.

'Thank you for helping Pa, Dungu,' Kerta said. He knew Dungu from the kampong near Anjer.

'He was right. The sea is different.' Dungu stepped sideways and examined the ragged cuts done by Kerta and Jan to the net.

'Did you lose this?' Kerta said.

Dungu looked at him and sucked at his lip as if trying to work out something. Then he made a soft sigh. 'No. It is not mine. But my net was taken by the ghost of the sea, Antoe Laoet. How much would you take for it?'

'Well, it's not mine, there is Jan.'

Dungu glanced at Jan and muttered softly. 'The Dutch boy will want gilders. A lot of them.'

Kerta called to Jan. 'Dungu wants our net – what do think?'

'Me? Oh, that net is all yours.' Jan shook his head.

Dungu looked at him. 'You're a different Dutch.'

'I was helping save the *Goliath*. That's all.'

Dungu smiled at Kerta. 'Fish, perhaps?'

'I don't know . . .'

Dungu squatted and waved his hand to bat down Kerta and Jan to his level. 'Now, you have to agree that it is not a good fishing net.'

'I suppose so,' said Kerta.

'Especially since you boys made a hole where all the fish

in Sunda Strait and a warship could get through.'

'I suppose so.'

Jan was looking at Kerta in annoyance.

'I mean, look at it. Nobody would want it.'

'It's not much.'

'Maybe I should ask for money from you to take it away.'

'I guess so . . .'

Jan was glaring at a pebble.

'Right then . . .'

'But you have no net,' Kerta said.

'Ah . . .' Dungu rocked back onto the balls of his feet and smiled. 'There you have me.'

Kerta smiled back. 'A little bit.'

'All right, what if every week I give you two good fish from my catch?'

'All right.' Kerta shrugged. Really, he couldn't expect anything better.

Dungu tilted his head and studied Kerta's face. 'But the fish is for your ma, isn't it? Maybe there is something for you.'

Kerta looked up.

'What about a top?'

'A top?'

'A new one. I'll find the tree and carve it out. All right?' Dungu offered his hand.

'Oh, yes, yes. Thank you.' Kerta grabbed his hand and shook it like it was a thrashing fish.

'It'll take a while.'

Dungu gathered the net, with Kerta and Jan helping, then he waved and walked away with the parts of the net trailing beside and behind him.

'A top?' Jan said with a grimace, looking at the back of the small fishermen. 'A toy for little boys?'

'This is different. You'll see.' And then Kerta remembered that he was Javanese and Jan was Dutch. They would probably not speak to each other again after his father picked him up from here. 'Ah.' He shrugged. 'Let's go up the lighthouse.'

'The Fourth Point. At last!'

the fourth point

JAN stepped past the red door and stopped. Kerta watched his face as he stared at the lighthouse interior and remembered how he had felt when he had first seen it, and smiled. There was only one wall, a round granite wall, but you expected that. What you didn't expect were the girders: red, thick iron girders set against the white wall, that divided the building from the concrete floor to the wooden ceiling into great wedding cake slices. It was as if there were two lighthouses – the white granite wall and the iron skeleton – racing each other to the beacon.

'A lighthouse?' Jan said softly. 'It's not a castle – it's a warship!'

Kerta frowned – now the Dutch boy sounded like him. He shrugged. 'You should hear the iron in a storm! Creaks and shivers all over the place.'

Dodging some tools, he skirted the ropes and lanterns hanging on the wall, and ran up the curved stone steps to the first ceiling. He deliberately thudded his head against the wood, forcing a small rectangle to lift, which he pushed up with his hands until it swung away.

He panted a little. 'The lighthouse has trapdoors all over the place, but Jacob lets us keep them all open – apart from this one. This one keeps the monkeys out of the lighthouse.'

Kerta began to climb. Jan followed. In the next section up, the girders met with more girders, and passed through another ceiling. A long window spread light across stacked bags and barrels. This level smelt of rice and kerosene. There was a bucket on the floor and a light cable reached from its handle to a hole in the ceiling.

'That's how we get oil, kerosene – even water – to the top,' Kerta said.

'Ah.' Jan grabbed at the cable and looked up at the hole in the ceiling. 'Oh, yes.'

Kerta nodded smugly. He knew what Jan was seeing – circles within circles until there was a spark of bright light. The first time it was as confusing as looking into a telescope. 'Now you can see how far we have to climb.'

Jan groaned softly as he followed Kerta up the curved red iron steps.

The next section smelled of tea and flour. Several bags and large tins were stacked under the steps.

'We had to stay here while Pa fixed the hut,' Kerta said. 'It wasn't too bad. But Dewi was very frightened when a big storm hit and the girders kept on creaking. She thought that Antoe Laoet was after her.' He grinned.

'Oh.' Jan looked blankly at Kerta.

'The Ghost of the Sea.' Kerta sighed a little and kept on climbing.

'Oh, them, they really are everywhere, aren't they?'

Kerta looked at him. 'They're not funny.'

'Sure.'

'Antoe Laoet almost got Bas. That's why he is frightened of the water.'

'He'd be frightened of a squawking seagull.'

Kerta frowned and pointed at the girders above. 'See that?'

Some of the red girders were short, but others were bolted to them to reach the ceiling. These were grey and a different shape. And the granite wall seemed to be lighter from there.

'Ah, yes . . .'

'That's because of what Antoe Laoet did a few years ago. We weren't there, but Jacob said that half the lighthouse fell over.'

'Fell over!' Jan stared at the grey girders, and turned to Kerta. 'Did Jacob say it was Antoe Laoet?'

'Tuan Jacob is Dutch. He said it was a storm, but it doesn't matter. Everyone here, Pa, Carver, the Brothers, the villagers in the kampong, knew that it was Antoe Laoet who knocked down the lighthouse.'

Jan slapped a solid red girder. 'It must have been a terrible night.'

'It would have made Dewi's hair go white – maybe yours too.'

'I don't get scared.'

'There's a worst thing than Antoe Laoet, much worse. A real monster.'

Jan shook his head. 'I am not frightened of ghosts. That's for the Javanese.'

Kerta pressed his lips together and kept climbing. They finally reached a small section where the cable fed into an oiled winch and complicated-looking machinery ran from floor to ceiling. A bright window lit a workshop area and a small store of kerosene lay to one side. A worn ladder was bolted to the shrinking girders and to two side-by-side trapdoors.

'That's the lantern room,' Kerta said.

Jan was looking at an elaborately carved teak cross on the wall.

'That was Carver's present to Jacob,' said Kerta. 'Jacob says that now the Fourth Point Lighthouse is better than the Anjer Church. But Jacob gave the lighthouse an even better present. I'll show you later. Those are ours.' He pointed at the rolled prayer mats under the cross as he pulled Jan to the final ladder.

One of the trapdoors was open and there were some sounds coming from the ceiling.

'Hey, Pa!' Kerta shouted at the trapdoor. 'I'm sending Jan to you, all right?'

There was a shuffling sound above the ceiling.

'You have a look.' Kerta pushed Jan. 'There's no room for three up there.'

'Come on, boy.' Pa's voice echoed around the area.

Jan climbed the ladder, at first slowly but he spurted towards the end. Kerta followed him and smiled when Jan stopped. He knew what Jan was seeing.

Jan had put his head into Pa's cage of shining glass. Pa was hunkered over the lamp, surrounded by plates of glass whose surfaces reflected a distant rippling sea and an endless sky. Each diamond held a picture – a fishing boat, a lonely island, a sea eagle – for a moment.

This was Jacob's marvellous magic machine. Pa was now working within the heart of it, wearing a linen apron to prevent himself from scratching the massive glass lens. The lens was taller than Kerta and would have needed two Kertas to join their arms around it. The glass of the lens was cut into elaborate shapes and Jan saw parts of his face reflected back to him. Pa's head would look fragmented in the heart of the lens too, but he wouldn't notice. He had more important things to do.

He was trimming five wicks in a brass lamp that drew kerosene from a reservoir below the lens. He finished his adjustments and slowly withdrew from the lens and closed the round section. As the sun set he would light the five wicks and a bright fire would blaze in the heart of the lens. The clockwork machinery down below would turn the massive lens, sending a brilliant white flash across the Sunda Strait for up to twenty kilometres, twice every twenty seconds.

'Do you like our lighthouse, Jan?' Pa wiped his hands on his linen apron.

Jan nodded.

'It looks better at night,' Kerta said from below.

'I know that. I saw it from the ship when we sailed in from Amsterdam.'

Kerta was annoyed. 'But you haven't seen it from the gallery. Pa, can we go outside?' The gallery was a narrow balcony curving round the glass panes of the lighthouse.

'Careful.' Pa was polishing the bullseyes.

Kerta moved to the second trapdoor, slid back the two catches and pushed his shoulders against the tar-painted door until it groaned away from the frame. When the trapdoor stopped halfway he clambered out.

At first Jan followed, but when his eyes adjusted to the open he almost stepped back down inside. Very carefully he eased himself out to the gallery, gripping one of the wooden frames that held the glass panes in place. His eyes locked onto the distance and he was awkwardly swallowing, like a trapped monkey. He and Kerta were standing on a wooden octagon rimmed with a thin, black iron railing.

A small carved lion leaped from the railing to the distant sea.

'That is Jacob's present,' said Kerta.

Jan's eyes wandered from the lion to the water. There was nothing between but a howling drop. His eyes jerked back to the lion.

'Well, the lion is Carver's work; he says it is an Arab lion. But Jacob worked out where the lion should leap. He has a globe in his bungalow showing everything in the world, so he worked things out and came out here with a compass. So that lion leaps past the edge of Sumatra, across the Indian Ocean to Mecca.'

'Oh . . .'

Kerta shrugged then saw Jan's fingers whitening on the frames. 'Great view, hey?'

Jan pressed his cheek against the glass and stared at the lapping jungle and the distant hills. 'Um, Fourth Point is high, isn't it?'

'More than forty metres. Dewi doesn't like looking down, either.'

Jan jerked his face from the glass and swung his body around in defiance. A warm blue sea stretched from the haze of distant eastern horizon, to the cloud-shrouded Sumatran mountains, to the rugged fortress of Thwart-the-Way Island. The sea was patterned with currents, breezes and small fishing boats. A lone steamship crawled towards Lampong Bay in Sumatra.

'Yes, it is a great view.' But there was a slight tremble in Jan's voice.

'Pa and me sit here like sultans.'

'I like it; I wish I could come here instead of my chalky school . . .'

'But you need nerves up here.'

Jan's pressed his lips together and stepped back from the thin railing. But then he grabbed it with both hands and wouldn't look down. He snarled, '*Your* Fourth Point? Anyway, why is called that? Fourth in importance?'

Kerta snorted. 'That's what the keeper of First Point thinks. He thinks his lighthouse is the most important in the Dutch East Indies. But that's not it.' He pointed south-east, past a hazy island. 'You can't see First Point – Java

Head – but there's where it is. At night any ship that wants to get into the southern entrance of Sunda Strait will look for Java Head, and the next lighthouse, Second Point. And then Third Point, and then you almost see – there's a bay – and then there's us. Fourth Point.'

'I think the keeper of First Point was right.' Jan smiled sweetly at Kerta.

Kerta walked around the gallery. 'Tuan Jacob says, All right, most ships bound for Canton, Hong Kong, Singapore and Batavia use the strait and most of them rely on Java Head, but he says for every ship going *up* the strait there is a ship going *down* the strait – maybe more. And *those* ships use us. And the ships that come from Java Head use us to steer away from Thwart-the-Way and maybe for getting to Anjer. Ships sailing for New York, Amsterdam, London, even Australia – drop in for the water and the coal. And there is more.'

Kerta pointed at a large white buoy closer in to the lighthouse. 'You see that?'

Jan nodded. 'Papa wanted to hook it when the net stopped us, but we couldn't. What is it?'

'There is a telegraph cable under there. It goes all the way from Telok Betong in Sumatra to here. And then it goes to Anjer. Java Head hasn't got anything like that.'

Jan crept his hands along the railing. 'Where's Anjer anyway?'

'Oh, it's there, you just can't see it. Just follow the other white buoys . . .' Kerta pointed.

His finger passed the small yellow river staining the blue strait about two hundred metres away, but he knew that river had a link with Anjer. If he paddled up the river for three metres he would find a jungle fork. That was Anjer River and if he paddled left he would be in Anjer in no time at all. The kampong was between the two rivers and they could see some palm thatches in the trees, but Anjer was hidden by little headlands and trees.

'That's it?' said Jan in disappointment. 'I thought I'd see my house.'

'Just too much jungle. Sometimes I can see the light from the Assistant Resident's house in the dusk.'

'Anjer doesn't look like much, does it?'

'Maybe . . .'

'And this lighthouse is nothing much. I've seen better ones in Amsterdam.'

Kerta glanced at him. 'You wouldn't know, you haven't looked down!'

Jan jerked his head down. And saw the sea rippling against stones and the white tower rising from them. And the thin rail began to shake.

'God . . .' His hands whitened as he tried to stop the movement. And then he caught Kerta's grin and saw Kerta's hands shaking the rail. He let go and stepped back. 'Oh, very funny.'

'You're as bad as Bas. Now you know how the keeper at Java Head felt last week. But don't worry; nobody has fallen from here for – perhaps a month . . .'

31

Jan read his face and ignored the last words. 'What happened to the keeper?'

Kerta walked to the eastern side of the gallery and stared beyond the misty island. 'He saw Orang Aljeh.'

'Eh?'

'That is far worse than Antoe Laoet.'

'Oh, another scary ghost.'

'Hey, maybe you whiteys do see ghosts too. Thwart-the-Way Island got that name because your captains thought a ghost had shoved it in the middle of that narrow entrance of the strait to make things difficult. And Orang Aljeh frightened the keeper of Java Head.'

'It wouldn't frighten me.'

'You were scared here!'

'That's different. What did he see?'

'A few days ago he said the water shivered and then became still, like it was glass. And then his lighthouse shifted. He said it seemed to come from Krakatoa.' Kerta pointed at the misty island.

Jan jerked around. 'What?'

'He said the lighthouse –'

'No, the place.'

'Krakatoa. There.'

Jan stared at it. 'That's it? We were going to it today.'

'What? Why?'

'Lloyd's Agent Schuit has an odd friend who wants to see it. Schuit had *Goliath*, but he couldn't leave his work in Anjer, so Papa offered to take the friend.'

'Stupid . . .' Kerta muttered under his breath.

'Because of your ghost, right?'

'Yes.'

'And when did you last see this ghost?'

Kerta hesitated.

'You have never seen it, right?'

Kerta looked at Jan's face. 'I don't need to see Orang Aljeh. I don't need to see Antoe Laoet. Every time I climb the lighthouse I see enough, and my Pa thinks about them every day. I don't know why . . . but I know the ghosts are in the sea and on Krakatoa, just like I know the moon pulls the tide. The ghosts gave you a warning this afternoon.'

Jan glared at the island. 'Ha! I'll be there tomorrow; I don't get frightened by old women's tales and wobbling pieces of metal.' He thumped the rail and the lion dipped. Kerta shrugged.

'I think your father is coming.'

A horse with a buggy was cantering over the river bridge.

'I've got to go.' Jan clattered down the ladder.

Kerta followed him, and Pa stopped oiling the light's clockwork to join them. They clanked and banged all the way to the kitchen, with Pa closing the trapdoor behind them. Ma quickly gave Jan his dried and ironed clothes so he could change back in the *mandi*.

Pa met Jan's father on the track and talked for a few minutes before walking towards the hut. Joost tapped the rim of his white cap when he saw Kerta and smiled.

33

'You're a good lad, Kerta.' He fished into his pocket and pressed a guilder into his hand as Jan stepped out of the hut.

Dewi beside Ma stared at the glinting silver.

Jan tossed Kerta's shirt at his head, muttering, 'He's not worth it.'

'You!' Joost prodded his finger at Jan. 'You don't jump out of a boat again.'

'But *Goliath* is fine, isn't it?'

'Yes . . . But –'

'We are still going out to the island?'

'Tomorrow.'

Jan flicked his eyes sideways. 'Why don't we take Kerta along?'

Kerta was still showing the coin to Dewi, but his eyes widened.

'Well, why not?' Tuan Joost smiled at Kerta.

'Ah, I'm not –' Kerta saw Dewi's watching eyes and his words died.

''Course he might be too scared. Too wobbly.' Jan smiled at him.

Kerta remained silent as he relied on his mother.

But it was Pa who shook his head. 'I don't think so . . .'

Kerta willed his lips not to grin.

And then Ma looked at Pa. 'Let it go, Ndora.'

Pa looked at Ma for a moment, then slightly lowered his head. 'All right. Thank you, Tuan Joost, for taking my boy. He will learn things on the island.'

Joost saw Jacob coming out of his bungalow and waved. 'We'll take care of him.' He nodded at Kerta. 'One o'clock at Anjer's Water Wharf, right?' He and Jan walked towards Jacob.

Pa murmured, 'I wasn't thinking of Krakatoa's Orang Aljeh. Only Antoe Laoet.'

Ma patted his hand. 'I know.'

kampong

IN the dead of night, Kerta quietly climbed down from the hut, walked to the edge of the keepers' area, then looked back. The huts and Jacob's bungalow were dark, but Fourth Point was a white tower against the shimmering sea. Suddenly the high lantern hurled a beam far across the water, but after a few seconds the light flicked off, leaving him alone in the blackness.

He wanted to go back into the hut and sleep, but then he heard the soft tinkle of Dewi's wind-chimes, and it almost felt as if she was watching him.

Reluctantly he turned away from the huts and walked quickly down the track onto the warm macadam of the Great Post Road. The Dutch were very proud of this road – it went through Anjer, to Batavia, to the other end of Java. But tonight their road was a quiet as a dead fish.

Quiet as Krakatoa . . .

Kerta hunched as he slapped his sandals down on the road to the bridge.

It's not so bad, he thought. Pa said last night that Orang Aljeh hadn't stirred for two hundred years. And even then

36

it was nothing at all. A little bit of black smoke reported by a couple of Dutch captains. People in the kampong had forgotten about it. Jacob said, 'A spirit on an island? More likely a spirit in a bottle . . .' Pa said he wasn't worried about the ghost on Krakatoa, only the ghost in the sea. So did that mean Antoe Laoet *was* worse than Orang Aljeh?

But the Java Head keeper said that his lighthouse moved. And the Javanese keepers say the spirit is walking on Krakatoa.

Kerta slowed down on the stained concrete bridge.

Bas had seen the ghost on this river, just a few bends away, and since then he had never been the same. And when he sees Pa they look at each other in an odd, special way.

Kerta stopped at the bridge, placed his hands on the cool concrete rail and listened to the murmur of the water.

Just about here, he and Bas had climbed aboard his father's old dugout canoe in the early morning to set out to explore the river. His father had said that this small river was a branch of the slightly larger Anjer River, but nobody in the kampong had been up there. So they had paddled off without telling anyone.

*   *   *

In the beginning the journey was dull, as they passed huts, penned ducks and fresh green rice paddies, but soon the jungle took over. The high trees touched each other across the river, making the forest and the water dark. As they pushed

37

into the blackness the water growled softly, while things hissed and ticked in the jungle. He wondered if there was a tiger in there and Bas wondered if there was a crocodile in the river. They were frightened by thunder from a storm and when a rush of screeching monkeys crossed the river above them. The trees shivered from the rain, but only a few scattered drops reached the ground beneath them.

Then they reached the fork, a broader area, where the main river was much faster. The canoe bounced over low waves and then raced into Anjer River without any help from the paddles. It looked like they wouldn't need those paddles all the way down and they would get to Anjer before lunch. They were laughing and singing as they reached the rim of the rice paddies, when round a bend a half-sunk tree appeared before them.

They shouted at each other, tried to get to the bank, but the current was too strong. The canoe crashed into a solid branch, while other branches swept them into the swirling water. Kerta grabbed the tree's trunk and saw Bas tangled in leaves and pulling himself onto a thick branch. Then the tree rolled.

Kerta scrambled onto the trunk and saw Bas disappear under the water. He watched for Bas to come up, but he didn't. Kerta hesitated for a long moment and then dived. He saw mud water, branches bending and leaves swaying in the current like fish, but that was all. He had to go up for air. He tried again, found nothing, gasped again, tried again – and found Bas's hand swaying in the water. He fought the tree for Bas for a long while, but finally he managed to pull him away and up the bank.

But he thought Bas was dead until Bas coughed feebly, opened his eyes and stared at Kerta. He said, 'I *saw* the ghost . . .'

✳   ✳   ✳

Kerta rubbed his hand on the concrete rail of the bridge and walked towards to the kampong. He could see Bas's family hut in the shadows of trees, but Bas hardly ever slept there anymore. His father had spoken with Lloyd's Agent Schuit and they had both thought it would help Bas get over his fears by working on a boat.

With a shrug Kerta continued down the road. At least Ma only wanted him to see Krakatoa once.

Kerta started to pick up a familiar rotten stench through the tang of old fish and drying rice around the palm-thatched huts and his mouth watered. The big prickly fruit, durian, was in season, and every hut in the kampong – from the beach to the headman's sprawling house – would be reeking like dead animals until late July. Nobody liked the durian's odour, but everyone put up with it for the taste. Even Jacob loved it, described the taste as 'rich, butter-like custard, with almonds, cream cheese, onions, brown sherry . . .' But he banned the fruit from the lighthouse area because of the stench.

Kerta forgot about Bas and began to wonder if he had made a good deal with that fisherman, Dungu. He should have said, forget about the fish, just give me durian! Except he wouldn't have agreed to that.

The other smells, fish and rice, wafted over Kerta from two separate parts. As if the kampong was split by the Great Post Road into two villages there – the rice people and the fish people. On the beach there were many *proas*, nets hanging from coconut trees, and a few ragged huts, but on the other side he could see goats, bullocks and ducks sleeping near the sprawling bigger huts. Beyond those was the gleam of rice paddies.

The kampong was still and he could hear some deep snoring from the nearer huts, so he was surprised to see a dim light through trees. He finally reached the light, a kerosene lamp on the step of a hut. The net that had trapped *Goliath* was spread in the open, with Dungu, his wife and the angry boy repairing it. Kerta started to greet Dungu, but he realised that the sound of his voice would not be wanted in a sleeping kampong in the middle of the night. Anyway, he didn't have time to chat so he walked past.

But he was seen. 'Hey, dog boy.' Soft call, but it carried.

Kerta turned around.

'Yes, you!' The angry boy hissed as he pointed his fishing knife at Kerta.

Kerta shook his head, and continued along the road.

'Dutch dog!'

'Hasan!'

Kerta heard scrabbling behind, looked back and saw the boy running at him and Dungu sprawling across the net. Kerta stumbled sideways.

He thought, What do I do, run down the road? And tomorrow everyone – the kampong, the lighthouse and Pa – will know that I ran. Doesn't matter, run now! The boy is going to cut me . . .

But he stood on the warm macadam and waited.

'Hasan!' Dungu was shouting.

The boy stepped onto the road and waved his knife at Kerta. The blade caught the moonlight.

Kerta lifted his bare arms. 'What do you want?'

'Why didn't you let the Dutch pigs drown, hey, hey?' The knife danced around.

'They wouldn't have.'

As Kerta shuffled away from the boy, a distant part was studying him.

I don't know him, I've never seen him in the kampong before. And that name, Hasan, it's different. He is lighter than the fishermen and he's got a funny accent, not quite the same as the fishermen of Sumatra and never Javanese . . .

'You lick their boots, your father –'

'You leave Pa alone!'

'See!' Hasan stabbed the air towards the lighthouse's abrupt beam. 'Every night he shows the Dutch the way to burn my country!'

'I . . .' Kerta faltered and stopped moving away from the angry boy. He didn't know what to say.

'Hasan.' Dungu grabbed the boy's shoulder and pulled him firmly towards him. 'Kerta is not your fight. He has given us our new net.'

'But –'

'Go back and get on with the net.'

Hasan hesitated with his knife still drifting.

'Go!' Dungu's finger stabbed the air.

Hasan glared at Kerta but lowered the knife and slouched away.

Dungu sighed softly as he watched him move away. 'Sorry about that, Kerta, he's an Aceh boy,' he said simply, as if that explained everything.

'Oh,' Kerta said, as if he understood.

'What are you doing at this late hour?'

'I'm going to Krakatoa.'

'Ah . . .' Dungu nodded. 'They say it is a good spot for fishing.'

Kerta stared at him. That is all?

anjer

As Kerta left Dungu he briefly forgot about the angry boy with his gleaming knife and a slow smile began to grow. By the time he reached the arched stone bridge that crossed Anjer River he was almost beaming. He looked upriver as if he might see the tree that sank the canoe, but it was gone.

Didn't matter. Back then Bas saw a ghost, maybe Antoe Laoet, pulling him into the depths, but that wouldn't happen to anyone today. Krakatoa was so safe that fishermen dropped their nets there!

Kerta crossed the bridge to the town of Anjer. The river marked where the kampong stopped and Anjer began. The stink of the durian was replaced by a scent of flowers. On the kampong side a *proa* builder had set himself up under some coconut trees and a few *proas* were moored in the slow river, while on the other side was Tuan Joost's depot, the water plant and some Dutch houses and flowering shrubs. Jacob said that Joost wanted to move the depot closer to the wharfs, but sometimes the depot stored gunpowder, so the townspeople refused.

The water plant was part of an old tradition. Ships had

been coming to the river for hundreds of years, before the kampong even existed. Portuguese, French, British, Dutch ships used to drop anchor in Anjer's Merak Bay and sink their empty water barrels in the shallows of the river to collect water. The water plant upstream was where they got their water from now, and there was a water tank right next to a wharf for the ships. And as well as supplying the Dutch, the Arabs and the Chinese in Anjer, the water plant supplied a lot of people in the kampong with water. The angry boy was probably drinking water from the Dutch water plant . . .

Kerta frowned.

What was his name? Hasan? What was wrong with him? Dungu said he was from Aceh. What did that mean? Just that it's at the top of Sumatra and they are always fighting the Dutch. So that's why Hasan hates Pa and me and probably Bas – because we helped the Dutch. And he's going to get angrier when he learns that I'm going with the Dutch to Krakatoa. But I don't want to go, didn't want to help *Goliath*, and I don't like that smug Dutch kid. Hasan called me a 'Dutch dog' and he's right. I should have pushed the Dutch kid from the lighthouse gallery . . . That would have solved everything.

Kerta exploded his fingers and then he picked up the tang of tamarinds coming from Anjer. And spices, coconuts, jack fruit, mango, bananas, plantains and flowers. If he wasn't really looking he might think that he was entering a tropical forest, but in among the trees moonlight was glinting off the tiles of Dutch roofs. He understood the Dutch growing fruit trees – apart from bearing fruit they kept the sun's heat from the houses and the roads – but he couldn't quite understand why the Dutch planted flowers – those could not be eaten! But Jacob said that Anjer was the most attractive harbour town in the Indies.

Kerta was now moving along the esplanade lined with *warigens*, massive drooping fig trees, and past the biggest house and biggest block of land in Anjer – and maybe all Java. There were enough trees around it to start a plantation, and more flowers than in all the rest of the town. The mansion was of white stone, with so many glass windows that it looked like a collection of lighthouses.

This was the house of Tuan Thomas Buijs, Assistant Resident, who always wiped his hands with a white handkerchief. He had visited Fourth Point and Jacob's bungalow twice.

Tuan Buijs's house backed onto the bay with its own wharf and he had his polished launch moored there.

Kerta left the Dutch houses and the *warigens* for the broad, cobbled Waterfront, the wharfs and the Pilot's hut. *Goliath* was tied up to the wharf beside a dim light. Kerta slowed down.

He had never seen Anjer like this. Apart from *Goliath*, the only signs of life were a single glimmer from a Waterfront shop and two tired men loading heavy bags from the coal bunker to a barge on another wharf. It was a ghost town.

Kerta softly moved to the glinting water tank and for

a moment he stood in the middle of the cobbled road. He could hear the men on *Goliath* muttering, the coal men grunting, the barge tapping the wooden poles of the wharf. Turning, Kerta peered into the shadows, past the Great Post Road to the low hill of the Dutch church and the cemetery. The white tombstones seemed to be moving, but it was nothing more than a breeze passing through bushes.

Kerta shivered faintly, turned back to the Waterfront and began to smile. Close by was Anjer Hotel with a veranda – the only veranda in town – and an awning. On this veranda was a glinting brass telescope. And that broke the image of a ghost town.

Like *Goliath*, the hotel, a shop and two houses, that brass telescope was owned by Lloyd's Agent Schuit. Of all his businesses in Anjer, Tuan Schuit was very proud of his position as an agent for the important London shipping insurance firm, Lloyd's, so he was called Lloyd's Agent Schuit.

All the shops in the Waterfront were sheltered by coconut palms – except Schuit's hotel. He had taken out the trees in front of the veranda so he could use his magnificent telescope with a clear view. There was only one telescope in Anjer that was better than it: the Pilot de Vries's in his station hut – his was bronze instead of brass. Once, he had let Dewi look through it and she had fallen all over the place in excitement, waving furiously at a ship several kilometres away. Lloyd's Agent Schuit had chained his telescope on his veranda ready to use early in the morning.

At the moment every respectable person was asleep, but

in a couple of hours Anjer would wake up.

Lloyd's Agent Schuit would go to his telescope – maybe today he might look for his *Goliath* before reading any flags from passing ships. He would write a message for Lloyd's of London and go below and have breakfast with the hotel manager, Madam Schuit, and the guest Master Telegrapher Schruit.

One day Pa was invited to the hotel for lunch with the Lighthouse Keeper Jacob Schuit and Lloyd's Agent Schuit and Anjer Hotel's Madam Schuit and Master Telegrapher Schruit. None of them were related to each other. Pa said they got away from the terrible confusion of names by not using them at all.

At breakfast Lloyd's Agent Schuit would pass his messages to Master Telegrapher Schruit and Schruit would take them to his office next door to the hotel – after he had finished his tea. Meanwhile Thomas Buijs, Assistant Resident, would be making sure that his huge flag was hauled up his mighty flagpole. Tuan Leewen, the Harbourmaster, would be strutting and clucking about new ships in the roadstead, Tuan de Vries, Pilot, would be fiddling with his boats to make sure that they were fit to go to any ship that might need him, Doctor Dillié would be cleaning his instruments, Imam would be singing from his mosque, keeping his eagle eye for dropouts – like Kerta.

Next door to the telegraph office, which was always last to open, Tuan Li Yang would be carrying a large carved Indian outside his general store. Captain De Jong, ship's chandler, the barber and other shops would open, while Tuan Baha would be grinding fresh beans in his coffee shop. In Anjer there were quarters – the Dutch Quarter, Chinese Quarter, and the Arab Quarter – but on the Waterfront there was a mixture of everyone. The Chinese shops would open at sunrise for any ship dropping an anchor in the roadstead. Only the Dutch opened at nine o'clock. Baha's Arab coffee shop seemed to be open almost all the time, gathering captains from passing ships, Chinese merchants, Dutch women, army officers, Arab traders, fishmongers . . .

Jacob said that Baha in his little coffee shop knew more secrets than an army of spies.

At the end of the Waterfront was a little mosque, and the Arab Quarter centred around that. Further on was the British monument, a grey plinth on the edge of the water that had been ordered by the Lieutenant Governor of Java, Thomas Stamford Raffles, in memory of Lord Calheart. But the British had gone. There was nothing left of the British apart from that monument and the grave of a British officer in the Dutch cemetery. Now the fishermen slung their nets over the steps of the monument and used it like a drying rock. But there was no trace at all of the French. Maybe the Dutch would fade away like that . . .

There was an Old Dutch Fort near the monument, a block-house framed by a mud wall and moat. Three sides of the moat were nothing more than ditches, but the other side was a deep canal. The fort was built to keep out the British and French, but it didn't work. There had been

French troops there, and British troops, and then the Dutch returned. There were no wars in Java now and the fort was deserted, but later in the morning the canal would be humming.

Schooners, junks and a fleet of *proas* sheltered on the canal at night. A drawbridge near the fort would lift at dawn to allow the bigger boats to push up to the Great Post Road Bridge and close with sunset. Just before the drawbridge lifted, the canal would be as noisy as the Anjer market.

There was a thin wire from the telegraph office that stretched from pole to pole over the Waterfront shops, past the little mosque, to the Old Dutch Fort, all the way to the Great Post Road Bridge and across the canal . . .

Kerta's eye caught the glimmer of wire above the office. He knew that Dewi thought that Lloyd's Agent Schuit was a wizard with his telescope, but for Kerta the real wizard in Anjer was Master Telegrapher Schruit.

Schruit would finish his tea, pat the white tufts of hair around his ears, take Lloyd's Agent Schuit's message into his polished office, and sit down in front of his brass machine. He would gaze through his glasses, crack his knuckles and touch the brass knob to make tiny sparks of lightning.

The lightning sparks quivered past the Waterfront and the Dutch fort, to the drawbridge, and along the Grand Post Road to Batavia. They scorched their way into cables in Batavia that plunged into the sea to Amsterdam, New York, London – or went the slow way under the white buoys to Fourth Point, to Telok Betong, to Sumatra, to Singapore and overland. And the tiny lightning sparks would spell out words from Lloyd's Agent Schuit and travel around the world to Lloyd's of London.

That was magic, worth more than a trick with a brass telescope, more than a flickering wick hurling a beacon of light across a dark sea – and maybe it was even as powerful as Orang Aljeh . . .

Kerta slowly grinned at the still Anjer and felt for a moment that if he clapped his hands it would erupt into life. He turned and began to walk along the wharf.

sunda strait

 HE saw Jan near *Goliath*. He was watching the coal barge as it coughed slowly from the wharf towards an anchored sailing ship.

'I'm here,' Kerta said as he approached.

Jan didn't move. 'I didn't think you'd be coming. Thought you'd be too scared.'

'I'm not.'

'All right.' Jan turned. 'We almost left without you.'

'It's not one o'clock yet, is it?'

'Doesn't matter.' Jan shrugged. 'See that ship, there? You know what it is?'

Kerta squinted at the anchored ship. Lanterns glimmered at the main derrick, the open hatch and the decks, showing the skeleton yards on the three masts. The ship was long enough to be a clipper, but between the main mast and the foremast there was a long black funnel. And there was the gleam of cannons on the foredeck and quarterdeck.

He said, 'Um, a warship?'

'Yes, yes, but it is a *German* warship.' Jan pointed at *Goliath*'s stern, where the Dutch flag drooped from a staff.

'When Papa heard that it was going past Krakatoa this morning he said we had to have a race. You would have been left behind, but Professor MacDougal hasn't arrived. We can't go without him.'

'Can you see him now?' Tuan Joost shouted from *Goliath*.

Jan saw a man walking out of the hotel. 'Yes, Papa, he's coming.'

'Better come down now,' Tuan Joost said. 'We don't want the professor thinking that we are impatiently waiting for him.'

Kerta followed Jan down to the landing. Bas was very carefully tipping a bag of coal into a bow compartment under the deck. Joost clucked when a small piece of coal escaped from the bag and Kerta hesitated to swing into the boat.

But Joost actually smiled and waved him aboard. 'Good lad. Are you going to save us again? Now we can go.' He snapped his fingers at Bas. 'All right, now.'

Bas turned around from the compartment to open a small firebox under the round boiler and shovelled some of the new coal into the firebox. A sudden flare of hot crimson played across his face as the boiler softly hissed. He leaped around the boiler, adjusted a small lever and smiled weakly at Kerta.

And that smile linked them. Kerta worked at Fourth Point while Bas ran *Goliath* and his smile was saying, Ah yes, the Dutch can build marvellous machines, but it's us that keep them going.

'Sorry, sorry.' Professor MacDougal clattered down to the landing, shrugged off a green rucksack and tumbled onto *Goliath*. 'Was talking too late with our friend, Lloyds' Agent Schuit, last night. Fascinating argument . . .'

Joost grunted and Bas whipped the stern line from the wharf bollard, padded his bare feet across the planks, grabbed the bowline, pushed *Goliath* from the wharf and leaped lightly onto the bow. Kerta felt the propeller shudder under his feet as Joost pulled a lever near the wheel. Joost spun the wheel until the launch was sliding towards the bow of the German warship.

'It's a lovely ship, isn't it?' Professor MacDougal polished his glasses.

Joost grunted.

The coal barge was nudging the side of the warship and the derrick lowered a cargo net down to it. On the deck seamen were tightening wires connected to the black funnel.

'I guess the *Elisabeth* is going to use its engine,' Professor MacDougal said. 'A pity. Schuit says that when the funnel's down, the propeller housed and all her sails are rigged it is a lovely sight. Like the *Cutty Sark.*'

'I want to see how she can go with the engine.' Joost yanked a cord and a loud steam-whistle blasted from the top of the brass funnel as *Goliath* passed *Elisabeth*'s bow.

'We're racing her to Krakatoa,' Jan said.

'Oh,' Professor MacDougal said in surprise. 'Now?'

'Now.' Joost blasted the steam-whistle again, put the

stern to and accelerated. The Dutch flag flapped at *Elisabeth* and a few crewmen looked up.

'I guess we need a bit of a head start.' Professor MacDougal smiled at Kerta. 'Schuit says she can do twelve knots.'

Joost snorted. 'Look at it! That is a warship, for heaven's sake?'

Kerta looked back, and saw the crowded masts in the stars, the long bowsprit, the white carved woman thrusting over the water, the green copper just above the sea. He *must* have seen it from the Fourth Point.

'It looks all right to me,' Professor MacDougal said.

'It is solid wood. That might have been all right in the Battle of Trafalgar, but now the Dutch Navy has iron ships.'

'I guess *Elisabeth* can struggle through. It still has eighteen cannons.'

'Cannons are from the last century.' Joost turned away from *Elisabeth* and followed the white buoys to the winking Fourth Point.

When the light caught the launch Kerta waved at the lighthouse, but he knew that no one would be looking for him at that hour. After the flare of light there was nothing more than the dim glow of the compass before the wheel, the red and green navigation lights and moonlight on the water.

Professor MacDougal tapped Kerta on the shoulder and pointed at a dark shape in the distance. 'Is that Krakatoa?'

Kerta stared at it. 'Yes, Tuan Professor MacDougal.'

The man sighed a little. 'Can we drop big labels? You're Kerta and I'm Mac, right?'

Kerta nodded.

He could see Krakatoa's unusual peak against the stars and for a moment he felt that it was waiting for him. But after a while he followed Jan in sprawling on the padded seats, and slept with the gentle throb of the engine in his ear.

*   *   *

'Now *that* is a warship!'

Kerta jerked his head up and saw Joost shaking Professor MacDougal – Mac – from his doze. Mac forced his eyes apart and blinked.

Joost pointed to the side. Now the stars were washed away by a sky of coral pink and the motionless water mirrored the glow. The Sunda Strait looked like something from one of Jacob's paintings, but a large grey ship was disturbing the quiet image. As the ship approached *Goliath* its tall funnel belched a cloud of white, its two paddlewheels churned the pink water into foam and Kerta could hear the *tiching-tiching* of the blades. When it turned sideways the dripping wheel dwarfed *Goliath*. A man in a dark uniform studied them from the bridge wing with his binoculars as crewmen were moving big guns around on the deck.

'I hope that gunboat is not going to sink us . . .' Mac murmured.

Joost looked sharply at him. 'No, no, it is Dutch. We are

Dutch.' He pointed at the flag on *Goliath*'s stern and then saluted to the captain on the bridge.

The captain ignored the salute. The ship surged past and turned towards Sumatra.

'That is *Berouw*,' Joost said. 'Frightening enough for you?'

Mac glanced at Bas, who was wiping his mouth with his arm. 'I guess it's all right for going up a river to shell a rebel village.'

Bas looked at Mac in surprise and quietly nodded.

Kerta stared at the retreating gunboat and realised that it had probably gone to Aceh. That Hasan had probably seen it in action; maybe the gleaming guns had fired at him. That somehow changed things . . .

'*Berouw* is not another rotting riverboat!' Joost snapped angrily. 'It is iron, unlike that wooden German rat trap, the Elisabeth. And you saw those guns – four heavy guns, not old cannons. Forget about crawling up a river, those twenty-eight crewmen have the mightiest warship in all the Sunda Strait.'

Mac looked beyond the stern. 'Where is the *Elisabeth*?'

'*Berouw* would race rings around that antique.'

'I can't see *Elisabeth* at all; can you see it, Kerta?'

Kerta squinted across the calm water. 'Not yet.'

Mac turned to the bow. 'Well, that's it – we beat it. Not much of a race.'

Kerta looked back and breathed a soft hiss.

Krakatoa was now a mountain. Dark green jungle clawed up severe slopes towards the high peak. There the small crater was tickling a golden cloud, as if the old volcano was remembering its past.

'She is very slow, isn't she?' Joost dismissed the warship with flick of his hand and concentrated on *Goliath*.

There was a long-sailed *proa* ahead and Joost nudged the wheel to avoid its course, but he didn't have to. The *proa* was as still as beach sand.

Kerta waved at the fishermen and realised that they were not looking around them or worrying about their sail. They were bending over from the *proa* to present a piece of rice and fish to the sea.

'What on earth are they doing?' Jan squinted at them.

'They are giving a gift to Antoe Laoet,' Kerta said.

'Your Ghost of the Sea? Why?'

'Maybe he will fill their nets today.'

Joost snorted.

'That's stupid,' Jan said.

'I don't know about that . . .' Mac said slowly.

Kerta looked at him in surprise, then watched the fishermen lower their nets. He thought about Pa, and about how he had been a fisherman and must have been like that, nodding at the ghost. It had changed now. Pa always looked down from the gallery of Fourth Point as if he could see Antoe Laoet at the bottom at the sea. As if Pa and the ghost knew each other. Maybe even hated each other . . .

Pa watched the Ghost of the Sea like a monkey watches a tree snake, but he didn't worry about the Ghost of Krakatoa, Orang Aljeh. And Kerta?

Kerta turned to the high island. He thought, I am not frightened of the Ghost of the Sea, I've been swimming too many times, but the Ghost of Krakatoa is different. I don't know what it is and I don't want to know. I don't want to wake it.

Goliath murmured past the *proa* and edged towards the long, low Lang Island. There was a cluster of islands and tiny isles around Krakatoa, but Kerta knew they were like Krakatoa – deserted. When the launch slid into still water it felt like creeping through a cemetery.

'There it is, all of it,' Mac said in satisfaction.

Kerta had to remember that Krakatoa was more than just that peak. The jungle-covered mountain was called *Rakata* – The Crab – then there were two other peaks as well. But he had never seen them until now. He had only seen Rakata, from the gallery of the Fourth Point, and thought of it as simply Krakatoa.

Now Lang Island had slid from away from the remainder of Krakatoa, revealing its other peaks, Danan, 455 metres high, and Perboewatan, only 120 metres high. Neither of these had the power of Rakata, which was 834 metres from the beach to the pointed peak – but to Kerta they added to the menace of Krakatoa.

Rakata, Danan and Perboewatan were like a great dragon sleeping in the still water.

Mac took a steaming mug of tea from Jan. 'Thanks. Did you know Krakatoa has *three* volcanoes?'

'Um.' Jan glanced at Kerta. He didn't want to show any ignorance in front of him.

Kerta nodded. 'That's what Rakata, Danan and Perboe-watan are.'

That surprised Mac. 'You know that?'

'Everyone in the kampongs knows that they were three islands with volcanoes a long time ago. Then they grew. Bas told me that.'

Mac frowned at Bas. 'You are a dark horse. Why didn't you say that before?'

'You didn't ask.' Bas shrugged.

Mac sighed. 'I am a geologist – dabbling in volcanoes – I am supposed to know those things, but people in kampongs . . . How do they know that?'

'My father told me and his grandpa told him . . .'

'And his grandpa told him, and his grandpa, and his grandpa . . . Yes, of course.' He slowly frowned. 'Now, how do we get to – ?'

There were harsh shrieks from the island. Kerta knew what the sound was – thousands of white parrots – but for one terrible moment he had thought that Krakatoa was screaming in anger – at *him*. He felt the beginning of a shiver and tried to control it, but it ran up his back, quivered along the back of his neck and slithered down his arms.

Mac looked at him in surprise. 'Cold?'

Kerta saw the tiny goosebumps on his arms, shook his head and quickly rubbed his skin.

Jan had seen Kerta's goosebumps too. He didn't say anything, just smiled lightly, but that was worse.

Joost slowed *Goliath* as it approached a black beach. 'Can you smell the spices?'

Kerta sniffed the air and picked up the scent of pepper trees in flower.

'I think there was a village here a long time ago. The local fishermen – from both Java and Sumatra – still come here for the spices and some of the wood. But nobody lives here anymore.'

'Because of the ghost?' Jan glanced at Kerta furtively.

'Ghost? Oh, that.' Tuan Joost saw Jan's face and the tension in Kerta's.

'Well, there was an eruption here, wasn't there, Papa?'

Mac caught the sly look. 'That was very little and it was in 1680 – two hundred years ago.'

'So?' Joost sounded annoyed.

'It wasn't worrying villagers here, a hundred years later. In 1771, after finding the east coast of Australia, Captain Cook anchored the *Endeavour* at Krakatoa. Maybe right here. And he mentioned the village, rice paddies and pepper groves. Plus he came twice afterwards.' Mac smiled at Kerta. 'He must've loved Krakatoa – and its ghost.'

Joost shrugged. 'But that village has gone now. That's one hundred years in terror of a ghost.'

Jan was watching Kerta's face, but Kerta didn't move a muscle.

Mac made a soft sigh. 'Maybe they wanted to live near a town. There were a few other people here after the village died.'

'Pirates and killers.' Joost stopped the steam motor. 'Bas . . .'

He jumped into the shallows and held the bow. Jan slipped into the water on the other side and took Mac's rucksack from him. Mac stumbled down, staggered a little and looked back. Kerta had his feet on the rail, legs tensed, arms coiled around the boat's framework, but he was staring at the towering Rakata and listening to the shrieking jungle.

Mac spoke softly. 'Kerta, would you like to stay with the launch? You could help Bas.'

The deckhand frightened of water stared at Kerta's face.

Kerta sprang from the boat, splashed through the golden water and thumped his foot on the black beach, as if marking a triumph. Jan and his father cocked their eyebrows at each other, but Mac was smiling.

the crab

Mac took his rucksack from Jan and joined him on the sand while Joost talked with Bas. Bas pushed the boat into the deeper water, turning the bow.

'Well, which way?' Mac said.

Thick purple flowers spread from the narrow black beach to palms, ferns and long grass. Beyond that were thick bushes, tangles of creepers and tall jungle trees. It would be hard to climb Rakata, but there was a gentler slope towards Danan.

'Maybe there.' Kerta pointed.

'Fine.' Mac started to shrug on the rucksack.

Kerta stopped him. 'Let me carry it.'

'You?'

'I am very strong.'

Mac tilted his head. 'Are you sure? All right, thank you, but I take over when you're tired.'

Kerta took the weight, wobbled and started walking towards the shrieking jungle. 'See, it's easy.'

'Ah-huh.' Mac clumped after him, leaving Jan to follow. 'Those bloody parrots, you can't think with that din. Some people say those birds gave the island its name. Listen to them, *karkataka-karta! – Krakatoa.*'

Kerta looked at the deep shadows in the jungle and faltered. 'I'm not frightened of the Orang Aljeh. I'm not afraid of anything.' But he knew that he was lying.

'I am afraid of everything,' Mac said.

Kerta blinked at him. 'You're scared of the Orang Aljeh?'

'Well no, I guess not. That's yours. But for heaven's sake, I am a Scot. We have ghosts in every misty glen, a monster in a loch. I've got a rabbit foot for good luck and I'm frightened of a black cat crossing my path.'

'A cat!' Kerta had seen them in the arms of some Dutch women.

'Black cats. Terrifying.'

Kerta nodded in sympathy as he surged into the jungle.

Jan caught up to them as they moved into a steep valley between Rakata and Danan. He was wielding a machete, but the undergrowth was getting easier as they moved into the immense trees. In the deepening shadows the dense bushes faded away as high branches carried fern gardens. But there were breaks in the jungle canopy where there were a few fresh tracks. One track led them to a bubbling stream with a bucket tied to a branch.

'Pirates!' Jan said.

Mac laughed lightly. 'Not likely with the *Berouw* chugging around. You Dutch dumped a few thugs here, but it didn't last. Probably fishermen after some wood and pepper, or Batavia's gunpowder-makers collecting sulphur. I guess this is where Cook got his water from too.'

The water smelt faintly sulphuric, but it was beautiful to drink. Mac was carrying a bottle of water in his rucksack but he emptied it to fill from the spring. While they were drinking the water the parrots began to settle down.

As they climbed to the saddle the air became heavy with the scent of spices. Kerta could see smaller trees in the tangle of jungle and fragments of an ancient house by the track. The track reached the saddle and kept on across the island, but they had to leave it to reach the top of Rakata. There were no more paths, only slippery, light stones.

Mac was fascinated by the stones. He selected a long one with a bright yellow stain and tossed it lightly in his hand. 'So light, like balsa wood. Pumice.' He threw it to Kerta. 'You see these round Fourth Point?'

'I've picked them up. They're good for cleaning knives.'

'Look at the holes. These rocks cannot sink, so the ones you've collected probably came from here. You probably picked up pumice from that eruption two hundred years ago. From deep under the ground.' Mac took the pumice from Kerta and put it in his rucksack.

They climbed slowly, with Jan ahead swinging the machete. After some time they could look through the top of the trees to the cone of Danan below them, then a cloud drifted across the peak of Rakata.

'Hope that moves,' Mac muttered.

But as they crept up, the cloud slid down and enveloped

them. They were groping though cold white fog where trees became skeletons, bushes were strange shadows and the sound of breathing was hollow.

'Any minute you'll see the ghost,' Jan whispered back to Kerta.

Kerta's foot stopped mid-step and his eyes had a hunted look.

'That's not funny, Jan,' Mac said.

Jan shrugged as he kept climbing. Then he stopped. 'What was that?'

Kerta had felt something with his feet and Jan and Mac had felt the same thing. The ground had moved. Not much, more like the slope had given a slight hiccup. For a moment they looked at each other.

Then Jan stumbled backward shouting, 'What's that?'

'Just a tremor . . .' Mac said softly.

'No, no, that!' Jan pointed to some thrashing bushes near him.

A snake-head – bigger than a goat's head – thrust itself from the bush and flicked a long, forked tongue at Jan.

He screamed, tried to turn and run, but he fell heavily to the ground. The machete twisted in the air. As the snake-head lunged towards him, he scrabbled back, kicking pebbles away.

Kerta caught the twisting machete, swung it at the lizard and roared. Its dark blue body turned, and it skidded across Jan's shins. It was longer than Jan, and almost as broad in its body. It scuttled down the mountain.

They all watched the disappearing lizard for a long, still moment.

'What was that?' Jan said softly.

'It's only a lizard,' Kerta said.

'A monitor lizard.' Mac nodded.

'But it was so huge . . .' Jan took Kerta's offered hand and pulled himself to his feet.

'They can be big; some of them are called dragons. But how did he get here?' said Mac.

'They can swim – for a long way.' Kerta steadied Jan. 'Pa said that when he was a fisherman he saw one several kilometres from shore.'

Mac nodded and looked at Jan's washed-out face. 'Hey, those lizards are only after fish, birds and rats. It wasn't after you. The tremor frightened it.'

But Jan shook his head and stared at Kerta's face. 'Um, thanks.'

Kerta shrugged and passed the machete back. He was remembering how the keeper of Java Head had felt the ground moving a few days before. The keeper had sounded a little bit scared in his shaking lighthouse, but here was far worse. That tiny tremble showed that Orang Aljeh was stretching and Kerta was on his island.

the peak

 MAC crouched, put his hand on the ground for a long moment and then slowly shook his head. 'Nothing now,' he said.

He took the rucksack from Kerta and they climbed again. The trees dropped away, leaving stunted bushes. They used those bushes to pull themselves to the peak of Rakata then sat on the edge on the crater, panting and watching the cloud above it drift slowly away.

The crater was tilted towards a large, cracked edge, like the spout of a damaged teapot. It wasn't big, neither in depth nor width. Kerta figured he could pitch a stone from his side to the other without really trying, and if a tall tree from the jungle was in the bottom of the crater it would almost touch the cracked edge. There were a lot of bushes and grasses *in* the crater and no sign of steam at the bottom. Rakata was a dead crab on a beach.

Kerta frowned at the bottom of the crater and realised that he was disappointed! Before, he was frightened to wake the Orang Aljeh as he tramped around his mountain, but *this* – it was like watching rice being planted.

But Mac seemed excited. He opened his rucksack, pulled out his bottle and a bag of nuts, passed them around, and then took an odd wooden box from the rucksack. He removed the black cover from a piece of glass in a metal mount, then slid a square wooden frame behind the box. He turned a knob and the glass slid from the box.

'Camera,' said Jan.

Mac pulled three light, connected pieces of wood from the rucksack, then screwed them to the camera and stretched them. He aimed the glass eye at the crater, then changed the square frame.

The cloud that had cleared Krakatoa was wafting south to Sunda Strait. The German warship *Elisabeth* was charging down the strait with every sail unfurled; the Dutch gunship *Berouw* was paddling into Kampong Bay; a slow, small Dutch mail packet, *Zeeland*, was nearing the Sumatran coast; and the fishing boat that *Goliath* had passed earlier was floating off Krakatoa. Thwart-the-Bay in the distance completed the view.

But Mac didn't see any of this. He was fiddling with his camera pointing to the closer islands, the island called *Verlaten*, meaning 'Lonely', and the scattering of about ten tiny islets between it and Krakatoa. Mac slowly frowned as he stepped back, then jerked his head about as if he was being attacked by sandflies.

'I didn't see it. I didn't see it!' Mac sat down.

'Oh.' Jan nodded wisely.

'I will listen to every old story carefully now. There is a

very old story in China called *Bawshou Rescues the Sun*. In that story the sun is taken from the sky, plunging the world into darkness. Rice begins to fail. There is an old Javanese book called *The Book of Ancient Kings*, and it says that in about 500 AD 'the mountain burst into pieces with a tremendous roar and sank into the deepest part of the Earth.' And there was flooding. Java and Sumatra were divided. The ash from that eruption would have darkened the entire world.'

Mac looked at Kerta. 'Maybe your ghost came from that memory.'

Kerta blinked.

'Krakatoa was far bigger than it is now. Very big. How big? Well, there is this one.' He stood up and pointed to the long island, Lang, which they had passed to reach Rakata. 'And that one.' He swept his flattened hand towards a small rocky island, Polish Hat, close to Lang. 'And that one.' He stopped his hand on the other side of Verbaten and the islets. 'Plus this one we are standing on. Now that used to be the size of the *old* Krakatoa . . .'

Kerta looked at Krakatoa. It looked like a ship's bow nudging towards reefs, but the ship was ten kilometres long and three kilometres across. Together with the islands, the old volcano would have been over thirteen kilometres long. And that meant . . . Kerta lifted his head and stared at a sea eagle way above him circling the sky.

'Must have been two thousand metres high,' Mac said.

'But it couldn't disappear.' Jan was uncertain.

'Bas's stories,' Kerta said slowly. 'They were true!'

Mac nodded. 'Must have been terrible.'

'Orang Aljeh is here!' Kerta looked around wildly. He had accepted that there was a ghost on Krakatoa, but that was tolerable, like knowing there are sharks in the sea. But knowing that the ghost was definitely here *now* changed everything.

'Hey, take it easy.' Mac batted him down. 'It was 500 AD! Fourteen hundred years ago.' He wobbled a pumice rock beside his right foot. 'This island we are standing on didn't exist then. It built itself up from the bottom of the sea after the end of the old Krakatoa.'

The rock rolled down the slope from Mac's foot.

'There's something happening . . .' Jan mumbled.

'It doesn't –' Kerta felt Rakata move under his feet. A quiver ran up his legs to his stomach, then he sensed a deep thump in the earth. His eyes followed Jan's wobbling finger to Krakatoa's lowest crater, Perboewatan, and a plume of white steam rising from it. A cannon blast echoed around the island and a cloud of white parrots shimmered from the slopes.

Orang Aljeh had woken.

the fishermen

For a moment Mac seemed nervous, but then he relaxed. 'Well now, that's something, isn't it?' Smiling, he propped up the funny wooden legs and aimed his camera at the hissing crater.

Some of the white parrots settled back in the trees, but most of them kept flying towards Java.

Looking at the rising steam, Jan said, 'Ah . . . shouldn't we go?'

'The eruption is too far away from here to be dangerous. Don't worry.' Mac clicked his camera and slid another frame into place.

Perboewatan cracked like thunder and a spurt of white smoke shot up half a kilometre.

Kerta felt the earth jolt and his face became sickly. I woke it. The Dutch and the English captain never stirred Orang Aljeh because it cannot smell whites. But the ghost can smell the Javanese boy on its island . . .

'All right, we'd better move on.' Mac took his camera from the wooden tripod.

Kerta and Jan snatched the three legs, folded them and

jammed them in the rucksack. Mac tried to slow them down as he crammed his camera onto the tripod, but then Kerta slung the rucksack on his shoulder and ran down the crumbling summit. He reached the saddle in a breakneck charge and was aiming for the anchored *Goliath* when he saw other people on Krakatoa.

He scrambled round a tree, caught a bush and skidded to a stop. The people – definitely fishermen – were walking down Perboewatan's western beach. They didn't seem worried about the erupting volcano behind them and one of them kept poking at the sand with a long stick. There seemed to be mist floating above the sand – maybe steam.

Kerta frowned at the men and then slowly twitched a shadow of a smile. It wasn't he who had made Orang Aljeh angry. It was *them* . . .

Suddenly there was a trench across the beach, about ten metres away from the fishermen, where before there had been nothing but flat sand. The fisherman moved quickly away as the trench heaved grey ash across the sand. They sprinted when it hurled black rocks at them. One of them was limping, but a couple of his mates helped him reach some boulders on the edge of the island. Kerta didn't see them after that.

He looked back to see Jan galloping down the slope, and Mac shuffling slower behind him. Kerta hesitated, but climbed back.

'What happened?' Jan rushed past. 'Forget something?'
'Yes.'

Mac wobbled from bush to tree as the island shuddered. Kerta caught and steadied him.

'Thanks,' Mac wheezed. 'Not used to this.'

Kerta placed Mac's hand on his shoulder, turned and began to climb down. Linked like that, they steadily moved to the saddle, through the pepper groves, the remains of the village, past the bubbling stream, through the dark jungle. And while they climbed down, the island trembled, shuddered, boomed and crackled. It sounded like soldiers were fighting to capture the crater. Mac took his hand off Kerta's shoulder as they reached the long grass and they hurried past the palms and onto the beach.

Goliath was bobbing in the deeper water ten metres from shore. Bas was pulling Jan up the side of the boat.

For one terrifying moment Kerta thought, They are leaving us here!

But then Tuan Joost waved them to the boat in a hurry. They splashed in the shallows and waded through the shimmering water to the boat. Mac was hauled aboard by Joost, Bas and Jan as if he was a sunfish. Kerta pushed the rucksack onto the boat and leaped, pulling himself onto the stern.

Joost stepped behind the wheel and yanked the lever. The propeller churned the water. 'Sorry about the deep water, but I didn't want to get caught . . .'

'That's all right.' Mac was examining his camera.

Kerta hesitated before saying quickly, 'There were some fishermen on the island. Very close to Perboewatan.'

Joost spun the wheel and frowned at Kerta. 'So?'

'One of the men was hurt.'

Joost looked at Jan. 'Did you see them?'

Jan shook his head.

'We better have a look,' Mac said.

Joost's face darkened, but he turned the steamboat towards Perboewatan. 'Where did you see them?'

'They were on the other side. Near Verbaten.'

'You mean I have to go through those islets? I don't know whether the *Goliath* can slip through the shallows.' But he aimed the bow at the narrow stretch between Krakatoa and Lang.

Bas shovelled coal into the firebox, looking away from the soaring pillar of steam on the island as they approached it. There were several quick booms as they reached the narrows. Jan glanced at Kerta's face. Kerta rapidly looked away, but Jan had caught his eye. Jan was wishing that Kerta had not said anything about the fishermen.

As *Goliath* cleared the point of Krakatoa's Danan Kerta saw several trees burning on the slopes of Perboewatan. But Mac was only interested in the crater where the thick steam and gas were pouring out vertically into the air. Bas just watched his scoop and his small furnace; he didn't want to look.

'There!' Kerta jabbed at a *proa* on the beach with nobody near it.

But Joost shouted 'Oh, Christ . . .' And he spun the wheel from the beach. A high water-spout was slithering across the shallows near the first islets.

'There . . .' Kerta's finger wandered helplessly.

'Good, they can get out by themselves.' The bow surged from the water-spout to the open sea.

'There's no sign of them around the *proa*. Maybe they can't get to it.'

'Shut up, Kerta.' Jan was staring at the water-spout.

It was a thin column, and it swayed like a cobra as it moved closer to the *Goliath*. Kerta felt its spray in his face, although it was over fifty metres away, and a low circular wave rippled away from it. The wave would reach the boat in a few seconds; it was too small to worry about, but it showed how close that water-spout was.

'I'm not going to take any more chances.' Joost shook his head and steered between Lang and Polish Hat as the wave rippled under *Goliath*.

Kerta looked at Mac.

But Mac pointed at a second water-spout moving on the other side of Krakatoa. 'They will have to look after themselves.'

Kerta watched dully as the spouts marched around Krakatoa like menacing sentinels. There is nothing you can do, he thought. Is there?

He was relieved.

the telegrapher

As *Goliath* moved away from Lang, the little mail packet *Zeeland* nudged closer to Perboewatan, hooting. A crewman was pulling a number of small flags between the mast and the stern, as if in celebration.

'What do the flags say?' Mac said to Tuan Joost.

He shrugged. 'Something about Krakatoa. But we know that, don't we?'

The corvette *Elisabeth* was still charging towards Rakata. It seemed ready to battle the blasting volcano. But then it slipped away from the island into the open sea and *Zeeland* disappeared behind Lang.

Most of the fishing *proas* in Sunda Strait were now sailing towards safe bays, but several ships were still moving towards the volcano. An American brigantine was sailing from Java Head and an old grain hopper was plodding past Thwart-the-Way – and the Perboewatan column of steam now rose eleven kilometres in the air.

As Joost and Bas steered *Goliath* across the strait, Kerta, Mac and Jan stared back. After a while the water-spouts disappeared and the explosions petered out, but the column of steam kept going, spreading at the top like a Dutch woman's umbrella. Halfway to Anjer, Kerta began to taste bitter ash as a fine grey dust slowly settled on the deck of the launch.

Jan wiped his mouth with the back of his hand, then made a face. 'Lloyd's Agent Schuit won't like that on his boat.'

Joost glared at him. 'Shut up, boy.'

Mac rubbed his finger and thumb together. 'Lava dust. Never mind – Bas can shovel a bag of it; it's very useful for polishing things.'

Joost grunted.

Just so long it doesn't get worse, Kerta thought.

The blue sky slowly became dull and milky as the sun faded to resemble a washed-out moon. Kerta picked out the Fourth Point as an off-white stick against the jungle and eventually the beam from it appeared as a pale spot through the falling ash. Normally the light would be turned off at dawn, but Jacob must have decided to keep it on during the eruption. As *Goliath* drew nearer Kerta thought he could see Pa on the balcony – no, it was two people. Pa and Ma were watching for him. Then he saw Dewi running around the balcony. Kerta climbed up to the top deck and waved at them until they started waving back.

Joost weaved through fishing *proas* that were paddling and sailing to the Anjer River or the canal, while Bas stopped stoking the firebox. *Goliath* gently nudged the Water Wharf and Bas stepped out to hold the boat.

'Interesting day.' Mac smiled as he shook hands with Joost.

Joost was looking past Mac at the telescope glinting from the hotel veranda.

Jan smiled at Kerta. 'Lloyd's Agent is worried about his boat.'

Annoyed, Joost nodded at the veranda. 'You better tell Tweedledum and Tweedledee what we saw, Professor, while Bas and I take *Goliath* back to the canal. Take the boys.'

Mac shouldered his rucksack, took Bas's offered hand to pull him from the boat and strolled down the wharf. Kerta and Jan trailed after him as the launch puttered away. There were two men on the hotel veranda, both watching Mac intensely. Lloyd's Agent Schuit was standing behind his brass telescope and next to him was Master Telegrapher Schruit, who looked troubled.

Lloyd's Agent stepped away from his telescope and leaned on the rail as Mac approached the hotel. Every time Kerta had seen him around Anjer he had a smug half-smile on his face – well, why wouldn't he? Pa said that if *he* was the richest man in Anjer, with Lloyd's Agency, the hotel, Captain De Jong's chandler shop on the Waterfront, two houses and a couple of *proas,* then *he* would wear the smug look too. But today Lloyd's Agent had lost his smug look.

Now he was studying Mac's walk as if that could tell him how serious things were. 'What did you see?' he shouted while Mac was still moving along the pier.

Mac shrugged and crossed the road.

'Is it as bad as it looks?' The Agent's heavy body carried his wealth, but his worn shirt and denim trousers didn't show it, and he had been burned by the sun into almost a Javanese.

Mac leaned back and called up to the veranda, 'I don't really know. But Krakatoa is alive again.'

Master Telegrapher Schruit, a younger, thin man, but with white tufts at his ears, moved to the rail. 'Why don't you come up here, Professor? We have to know.'

Mac nodded and steered Jan and Kerta into the busy bar, up the stairs and out on the veranda.

'I knew it was Krakatoa,' the Telegrapher said bleakly.

The Agent smiled weakly. 'He's joined us now. He bought a house near the river and tomorrow he will have to rebuild it.'

'If the volcano lets me.'

'Ah,' said Mac. 'I think it will be like any other volcano around these islands – smoke a little bit and go back to sleep.'

'I hope you're right,' the Telegrapher said. 'My wife and children are sick and tired of hanging on in Batavia. She'd blame *me* for the eruption!'

Kerta looked up at him in astonishment, but then realised he was joking. He drifted towards the brass telescope and looked through. At first he was alarmed when he saw black smoke pouring from his lighthouse, but he quickly realised the smoke was not coming the lighthouse; it was coming from Perboewatan.

The Telegrapher pulled his brass watch from his waist-coat. 'What's the time – four o'clock? I'd better tell someone. Will you come?'

Mac, Jan and Kerta followed him to his office. He waved a lean operator away from the brass machine, jotted a few words on a notebook and passed them to Mac. 'Is that right?'

Mac showed them to Jan and Kerta and returned the notebook. 'That's fine.'

Kerta thought that his word for Krakatoa looked funny but he didn't say anything.

The Telegrapher flexed his fingers, crouched before his brass machine and tapped the polished knob, creating tiny lightning sparks. Up the wire, to the poles, through the Chinese Quarter, the Arab Quarter, the Dutch fort, across the main bridge, along the Grand Post Road to Batavia, to cables along the dark bottom of the oceans, to Amsterdam, London, New York.

The tiny lightning sparks said, *'Krakatan casting forth fire, smoke and ash accompanied by explosions and distant rumbling.'*

ghosts

MAC touched the Telegrapher's scribbled note and slowly frowned. 'I think I'd better go to Batavia, to tell them what's happening.'

'Oh,' Kerta said quietly.

Mac looked at him and patted his shoulder. 'Just keep watching your ghost, see everything. I'll be back.'

The Telegrapher and Mac wandered to Lloyd's Agent on his veranda, leaving Kerta and Jan to drift away. There were a few Dutch people bustling around the Waterfront, like Harbourmaster van Leewen poking his Meerschaum pipe at people, Pilot de Vries pushing his steamboat off the beach to reach a slow-moving ship and Dr Dillié hurrying past with his battered bag . . . Those people hardly glanced at the column of smoke, as if they had decided that it was nothing to do with them.

But there were a lot of people – Dutch, Chinese, Arab and Javanese – just standing still and staring. As Tuan Joost and Bas walked from the canal they were hounded by worried men. Kerta could see Bas throwing his arms about.

'They should have asked us,' Jan said. 'We've been *up*

Krakatoa. And saw the giant lizard . . .' He looked at Kerta. 'Are you going to tell a lot of people about that?'

'What?'

'You know . . . that lizard.'

'Oh.' Kerta tilted his head as he studied Jan's face. 'No. It's your story.'

Jan almost beamed at him. 'Hey, you want to go to my house? Just over there.'

Kerta's eyes followed Jan's pointed finger to a slightly pink house at the end of a street. 'Um . . .' He had never seen the inside of a Dutch house, apart from Jacob's bungalow, and he would love to see inside, but . . . 'I better get back to the lighthouse. Or Ma will feed me to the fish.'

Jan looked disappointed, but he smiled. 'You *too*? Next time, hey?'

They separated as Tuan Joost collected Jan, and Kerta walked towards the kampong.

On the way Kerta saw an old woman throwing mud at herself and at the edge of the village some men were staring through him, as if they couldn't see him at all. A ragged man ran past him, hissing like a kettle on the fire. A young woman was sitting on the step of her hut, her face streaked with tears and her hands squeezing each other. A goat was looking at her, its head cocked as it slowly chewed grass.

Kerta frowned and called to a man pulling his *proa* out of the water. 'What happened?'

'What happened? Have you no eyes? Look at the sky!'

The man pointed as he disappeared.

'But . . .' Kerta had been on Krakatoa and it wasn't all that terrifying. And the Dutch were almost ignoring it.

He was shivering in the road until he saw the goat had turned its head to him. It blinked.

The goat isn't worried about Krakatoa, he thought. The Dutch aren't worried about Krakatoa. It's only the Javanese who are frightened. The stupid, panicky Javanese – stupid, panicky us!

Kerta accelerated through the kampong, scattering a few ducks. He wanted to get away from the frightened people, to have his family surrounding him with that indestructible white lighthouse. But then he saw the angry boy, Hasan, crossing the road ahead. For a moment Hasan and Kerta stopped in the road and stared at each other.

Kerta was almost hearing the *Berouw* sound of the paddlewheels, *tiching-tiching*, as it moved towards him. With those four gleaming big guns. Hasan might have seen them fire at him . . .

What could he say?

But Hasan shook his head and walked quickly into the inland kampong area.

Kerta opened a hand in release as he continued down the road. He could see Hasan as he walked, through the dark filtering of some trees. Hasan was approaching two large huts when he shouted excitedly and ran under another hut. A shadow lunged towards him, grabbed him and swirled him around. Kerta saw a glint of teeth, then the shadow moved into the light, showing a man grinning. Then he stepped back into the darkness.

Kerta shrugged and walked on.

*　　*　　*

Jacob was talking to the other four keepers outside his bungalow as Kerta came home, and called him over. 'Were you there when it happened?'

Jacob asked a lot of questions and his twins came out of the bungalow with their amah, Rara, to hear him. Surly Dirck even stopped thumping Adam. Pa studied Kerta's face, Carver stopped wiggling his ears at Rara and the quiet Brothers stared at Kerta as if he was growing another head. Kerta talked while the light faded and a blue sun sank in the sea. He finished his story with the fishermen.

'They will be all right,' Pa said. 'They know what to do.'

Kerta just looked down, but Pa's words helped.

Jacob turned to glowing Krakatoa. The sky above it was reflecting a deep red. 'Well, we know what to do, don't we?'

The men grunted and Carver made a face as he walked with Jacob to the lighthouse.

'It's going to be hard work for a few days – maybe a week.' Pa shrugged at Carver, waved to the Brothers and walked to the hut with Kerta. 'Carver doesn't like work much. That's all right, the Brothers make up for it. Jacob wants the light on all the time until Krakatoa stops, and he is right.'

'Is it going to get worse?' asked Kerta.

'A bit. We will have to clean those lighthouse glass panes often because of the ash. Your fishermen have given us hard work.'

Kerta stopped on the steps to the hut. 'Because they woke Orang Aljeh?'

Pa smiled.

'I thought I did it,' Kerta said bleakly.

The smile died.

Dewi ran to the steps. 'Aren't you coming?'

Pa nodded to Dewi and Ma as he pushed Kerta up to the veranda.

'The island looks very hot.' Dewi nodded.

'Well, it was . . .' Kerta caught Ma's eye as she passed him a bowl of fried rice and his voice petered out.

'The island just looks like a stove,' Ma said quickly.

'So long as it's a long way away . . .' Pa said and sat at the table with Kerta.

Kerta felt the steam of the bowl on his face and somehow he began to feel safe. He could remember the explosions, the shaking of the ground, the shoots of steam and he could *see* the glow of Krakatoa, but he could feel the bowl under his fingers, and taste the rice and egg on his tongue. And that made all the difference. The bowl and Pa, Ma and Dewi were real – Krakatoa was in the past, like a ghost . . .

Pa nodded at the red sky. 'You didn't do that, you know.'

'All right.'

'The fishermen didn't do it either. Orang Aljeh and

Antoe Laoet don't care about us. They do things just because they can.'

Kerta looked through the rice steam to Krakatoa. 'I guess it wasn't all that bad on the island, Pa. Especially when we were a little way from it. But a lot of people here are very frightened of the volcano – a lot of our people, Javanese . . .'

Pa looked at him.

'The Dutch don't get frightened; they just look at it and keep on going. Their ships never turn back. But the fishing *proas* run. There's not one of them left on the strait now.'

'Maybe they know more than the Dutch.'

Kerta saw the brilliant beacon of the lighthouse casting its light far across the strait. It was just a few wicks and a fantastic lantern. He thought of the *Berouw* paddling past with its grey guns, *Goliath*'s firebox pushing smoke up the brass funnel to get its propeller going, and Master Telegrapher Schruit's tiny lightning sparks that sent messages round the world.

He thought, The Dutch can do anything, so they don't worry about a little volcano. The Javanese cannot do anything, so we have to watch very carefully.

Pa looked at him. 'My father told me about the island erupting. Not the small eruption. This was one his father told him about, and his father told him, and his father, his father . . . Before the Dutch. The Dutch say this is just a story. That's all right, I know that it happened and that's all that matters.'

'Mac – a professor who came with us – said there was an explosion. An enormous one, a long time ago.'

'He said that?'

'He said he was a geologist and could see the signs, and he had read an old Javanese book.'

'And he didn't get scared today?'

'Not really. He wanted to stay there. Jan and me had to pull him away.'

Pa shrugged. 'So he believes in an eruption, but he won't believe that it can kill him. There are no ghosts on his island. Your professor is the same as the Dutch and some women . . .'

Ma looked at Pa as if he was a cockroach, but she didn't say a thing.

'They don't think that there are spirits in the sea, in the mountains, in the rocks.'

'That's not –'

'We men can feel Orang Aljeh and Antoe Laoet beating in our blood. All the time.'

'But you didn't feel Antoe Laoet that time . . .' Ma said slowly.

Pa dropped his head, and for the first time Kerta could see pain on his face.

'I am sorry,' Ma said quickly. 'I shouldn't have said that.'

Pa waved her words away. 'Doesn't matter. It's a long time ago. I've got to clean the panes . . .' He turned and left to climb the lighthouse.

*   *   *

Kerta woke to the quiet creaking of the hut but no gentle rumble from Pa's snoring, which meant he was still working at the lighthouse. Kerta was very tired; his leg muscles throbbed, and he could feel many tingling scratches, but he was awake now and he knew that he would not go back to sleep. He shrugged, got up and crept out of the hut.

He went to the lighthouse and found Carver sending up some kerosene via the cable on the second level. He looked worn out, but his knife was on a barrel with a piece of wood. He could carve a dancer in a week while he worked in the lighthouse.

'You're helping?' Carver said. 'Good. He's up on the gallery. With Jacob.'

'Thanks.' Kerta kept climbing.

At Fourth Point there were special things, like calling the Master Lighthouse Keeper just 'Jacob' because he liked it, or calling Budi and Wayan 'the Brothers' because they lived, worked, fished, laughed and sang together. The Brothers put on a shadow puppet theatre, *wayang golek*, at the Anjer market, using Carver's puppets and getting Baha from the coffee shop to tell an old Arab tale. Carver was called 'Carver' because that was what he did – carved wooden objects. And at Fourth Point Pa was the second-in-charge because that was so. Carver was older than Pa, the Brothers were faster and stronger than Pa and all Javanese lighthouse keepers had the same rank with the same money, but everyone from Jacob to pesterer Dewi knew somehow that Pa was the man to see. Everyone, apart from Ma . . .

Jacob was pouring kerosene into the wicks' container as Kerta arrived. 'Good, good. Your pa's out there; give him a bucket of water. It's getting worse.' His white whiskers glinted as he nodded and spoke.

Kerta filled a bucket from the tank near the machinery, added a touch of vinegar and carried it to the gallery. The smell of sulphur was stronger here and ash was drifting over everything – the rails, the deck, the trapdoor, the framework of the panes. When the beam clicked the night seemed to be alive with millions of insects floating down to the water.

Pa wafted from the shadows and took the bucket of water from him with a low grunt. He lifted a scrubbing brush from the dirty water in a second bucket and tipped this bucket over the edge. Kerta moved to take the empty bucket, but Pa waved him away.

'Later.' Pa looked at Kerta for a bit and then used his brush to attack the clinging grey ash on the window panes.

Kerta grabbed a large rag from the rail and, turning his eyes away from the glare of the light, wiped the rag over the surfaces Pa had scrubbed.

As Pa finished one of the panes he looked at Kerta. 'I don't think that you knew what we were talking about in the hut. When Ma said that I hadn't felt Antoe Laoet.'

'Um, no.'

'Once, I lived in a fishing village, Lebak, with my parents, and an uncle, and a grandfather – a lot of people.'

'You never talk about them . . .'

'This is why.' Pa scrubbed at the glass. 'I was working in a *proa* on the Indian Ocean, a long way from Lebak. We could see the mountains of Java, but that was it. We had presented Antoe Laoet fresh fish with fried rice and eggs. I will always remember that. Then there was a bump. It was nothing – a ripple. We didn't see it coming. A swell of one metre – no more – passed under our *proa* and was gone, as if Antoe Laoet had belched. We didn't think about it.

'Except for an old fisherman. He stared at the swell as it raced from us – as fast as a storm cloud streaking past the moon – towards the shore. And he said, "That is bad trouble, we should go back to the village *now*." He was laughed at and we fished until the *proa* creaked with the load. But the old fisherman was right. The rest of us didn't feel anything, but with his thin blood he had felt Antoe Laoet moving.

'When we reached Lebak, it was gone. The huts, the ducks, the goat, most of the people – your grandparents – my pa and ma. That one-metre swell had become a wave as tall as a hut. It charged from the sea, ripping everything apart and dragged it all into the muddy water.'

'I'm sorry . . .'

'It's a long time ago.' Pa lifted his head towards the red glow of Krakatoa. 'No, it's yesterday.'

Kerta looked at him uncertainly.

'Doesn't matter, Kerta. I'm like the old fishermen – I feel Antoe Laoet and Orang Aljeh. The Dutch can stroll around Anjer like sultans, but I can feel the mountain, and it's moving.'

the runner

 TUESDAY was nothing. Jacob and Carver left the lighthouse deep in the night and when the Brothers took over, Pa and Kerta went back to the hut. Kerta sagged to his palm mat, heard Pa's rumble and dropped off.

When he woke up, Dewi led Jacob's twins to him. They wanted to ask more questions about the island and Dirck forgot his normal sneer. Kerta had become the celebrity around Fourth Point, but Krakatoa was still pouring ash into the sky so he climbed the lighthouse with Pa in the afternoon to wipe the panes. Ma and Dewi wandered off to Anjer market, passing beached fishing *proas* on the way. At the market Ma learned that a convict had escaped while working on the Great Post Road. She said she had a feeling that she wasn't being told everything. Kerta thought of telling her about the man he had seen in the kampong, but it didn't seem important enough after Krakatoa.

* * *

91

Wednesday was better. Krakatoa cracked a few times, the fishing *proas* were still lying on the beaches, but Jacob told Kerta to stop cleaning the panes and sent him to Anjer for news.

As Kerta walked into town he saw Master Telegrapher Schruit on the hotel veranda with Lloyd's Agent Schuit's spyglass in one hand and a ladies' parasol in the other to protect himself from the drifting ash. Kerta was about to wave to him, but he suddenly swung his glass from the sea, aimed it at Kerta and beckoned to him. He came down from the veranda still carrying the parasol. Kerta was hoping that nobody he knew would see him.

'You were worried about the fishermen . . .'

'Ah, yes . . .' Kerta hunched a little and waited.

Master Telegrapher Schruit saw his face. 'It's all right. We had a message from Sumatra, from Willem – Controller Willem Beyerinck of Kalimbang. You know of him?'

Kerta nodded. The number of Dutch people around the Sunda Strait was so small that he knew of almost all of them. Tuan Beyerinck lived across the strait with his pregnant wife and two boys in the small fishing kampong of Kalimbang.

'Well, Willem said that eight fishermen from Sebesi Island were on Krakatoa when it started.'

Kerta smiled. 'They were the ones.'

'They said the beach was erupting, with fiery stones

92

and ash coming from the sand. Willem said that his wife, Johanna, didn't believe them, couldn't believe that a *beach* could erupt, so Willem went to Krakatoa for a look. The fishermen were right.'

'I know.'

'The fishermen had run from the erupting beach and splashed into the water and waded to one of those tiny islets for safety. Then Perboewatan quietened at night and they sneaked back onto Krakatoa, reached their *proa* and paddled quickly away, back to Sebesi Island and Kalimbang.'

Kerta slowly smiled with relief. He thanked Telegrapher Schruit and asked if he had other news about Krakatoa, but that was it. Ships were still going past the volcano and the volcano was still erupting. But there were fires on the island.

Kerta left Telegrapher Schruit and was turning back to the lighthouse when he saw Jan walking from the church area, carrying a few books under his arm. Kerta began raising his hand to wave, but then stopped. He thought, This is his town, Dutch people, Dutch kids, and maybe he doesn't want to be seen with a Javanese boy . . .

And then Jan saw Kerta, waved and yelled. He almost ran down the street to him. 'What's up?'

Kerta shrugged. 'Finding out what is happening.'

'Krakatoa? I had to go to school, but the teacher was so scared of it that we were let go. Hey, I am the hero because I was there. I even told them about the huge lizard – um, with a few changes.'

'You should have seen Dewi's face when I told her about the booms.'

'What're you doing now?'

'Oh, maybe heading back to Krakatoa. It looks like it's calming down.'

'You're not! Oh, funny kid. But Mac does think it's running out of steam. He's left for Batavia . . . Hey, you want a drink at my house?'

'Sure. I like –'

'Kerta!'

Kerta turned and saw a short man coming from the town market with a bundle of jackfruits and a light cord. 'Hey, Dungu, how's the fishing net?' Thinking: He is going to change the deal. He wants *me* to fix the net.

'Bad days for fishing,' Dungu said, opening his hand in defeat.

'Nobody is going out.' Kerta realised Jan was watching.

Then Dungu smiled. 'So I went into the jungle instead.'

'To be safe from the volcano?' Jan said.

Dungu frowned. 'To find the tree that is hiding Kerta's top. I found the top in an old teak tree and I have almost finished with the carving.'

Kerta's eyes widened. 'Does it fly?'

Dungu tapped the thin cord. 'I'm about to find out.'

'Can I –' Kerta glanced at Jan for a second and then made a slight shrug. 'Can I come along?'

'I thought you might.'

Kerta turned to Jan. 'I'm sorry –'

But Jan was talking over his words. 'Can I come too?'

Dungu's eyes shifted. 'But you are . . .'

Jan looked at him.

'Why not?' Dungu smiled at Jan and led them through the flowered Dutch quarter and into the village. A few people in the village looked at Jan, but he didn't seem to notice and kept on talking about Krakatoa – especially after Dungu had admitted that he had not been there at all.

Dungu's hut was slightly away from the road, but it had a good view through the scattered coconut trees to the sea. It was one of the smallest huts in the village – a matted room on short stilts – but Mrs Dungu kept it so trim, swept and washed that the captain of the *Elisabeth* would have felt at home. Mrs Dungu chopped open a green coconut for both Kerta and Jan, but she was mostly looking after Jan. Kerta accepted this – he knew that in her hut, Jan was royalty.

But to Dungu and Kerta, royalty was the carved top. Dungu gave Kerta a single peacock feather before going into the hut to get the top and he didn't need to explain. Kerta crouched down near the hut and began to sweep the feather gently over the hard earth, moving tiny pebbles and filling the slight depression left by them.

Jan sucked at his coconut, and watched in fascination until he was distracted by some movement down on the beach. 'What's that, then?'

'What?' Kerta was still concentrating on the ground.

There was a dull shout and murmur that came from a shuffling shape on the sand.

'That.'

Kerta lifted his head. 'Nothing much.'

The day's light was dying but he could see men were moving to the water. The men broke into two groups on the edge of the shallows, the larger group forming a crescent on the sand as if to force the smaller group into the sea. The small group splintered again, until one man was left in the shallows. He splashed slightly away from the others and stood motionless with his arms folded. The water shimmered with a bloody glow from Krakatoa. And then Kerta realised that he knew the single man – it was the same man who had been waiting for Hasan, the angry boy, in the shadows.

'Now, we'll see, eh.' Dungu padded down the steps with the top wrapped in an old rag.

Kerta turned from the man and moved away from the swept ground and Jan followed him, although he kept looking back. Dungu took off the rag with a flourish, flattened his left hand and put the top on the back of it. The top looked like two large plates pressed together, but in dark wood, with the dull point resting on Dungu's hand. The top was quite still with nothing at all but that point touching Dungu's hand.

'Look at it!' the man in the shallows said, and swung his arm to the glowing volcano.

Kerta ignored the man. 'It looks good, very good.'

'We'll see.' Dungu slowly wound the thin cord around the groove on the edge of the top.

'It's not going to go away, you know that!' The man shouted.

96

'Now . . . Ahayee!' Dungu lifted the top over his head, hurled it towards the swept earth and jerked the cord away. The cord cracked like a whip and for an instant the top spun in the air above the ground. Then it touched, wobbled a little, settled down and hummed softly.

'Krakatoa will stop you from fishing for a week, a month,' the man shouted. 'And when you finally get out there you won't find any fish because the volcano has frightened them off.'

The men on the sand growled.

Dungu frowned. 'Ah, fish are fish. I think the top rides well.' He squatted close.

Kerta carefully settled down on the other side and with a loose shrug Jan flopped to the ground, sprinkling grains of dirt on the top. Dungu and Kerta glared at him.

'I think it's good for an hour – at least.' Kerta said.

'It's got a bit of wobble, but I can fix it.'

'But that's not all, is it?' the man shouted. 'Look at it. That blazing mountain is getting angrier. It is building up . . .'

Dungu tilted his head as he watched the spinning top. 'They say that a storm is the ghosts of old medicine-men hurling their tops.'

'Krakatoa will drive us out of our huts and sink our *proas*. And who's causing it?'

Dungu smiled at Jan. 'The lightning is the whipping of the cords.'

Some fishermen were calling, 'Orang Aljeh!'

'And thunder is the medicine-men's tops.'

Jan looked at the face of Dungu and at Kerta who nodded. 'Oh, another one.'

The man shouted: 'Yes, yes, Orang Aljeh is furious – angrier than ever. Worse than that time two hundred years ago, even worse than that time the ancestors remembered.'

For a moment Kerta felt his lips twitch. Jan caught his expression and smiled back. Kerta looked at the top, slightly annoyed.

'But what has made Orang Aljeh so angry?'

The men on the sand shuffled and murmured as the top purred on the ground. Dungu lifted his head and gazed over at the man in the shallows.

'The Dutch!' The man punched his fist into the air. 'The Dutch – they sit on our land like a fat elephant in the mud. Sucking up everything that we have and squirting it over their wrinkled backsides. They're always there, counting your fish, your sacks of rice – and never mind about what you want to grow in your paddy; you have to grow indigo for their blue clothes . . .'

Kerta could hear the men mumbling over the creaking coconut trees. Dungu looked sideways to Jan.

'Now the Dutch have walked on Krakatoa and woken Aljeh –'

The men growled.

Jan hunched, and bit his lip.

Kerta hissed, 'But it was the fishermen who were on Krakatoa!'

'It doesn't matter, now.' Dungu shrugged. The top spun quietly on the earth between them.

'Orang Aljeh is angry with the Dutch,' the man shouted. 'But that's not all. He is looking out and seeing what happened to his Sunda Strait – crowded with foreign ships – and the beach with a Dutch port. And then you have the lighthouses, blazing at him through the night. Look at Krakatoa, look at the fire. He is furious at you – yes, you!'

Some of the men began shouting.

'Because you allowed it to happen. Remember Diponegoro!'

The fishermen yelled.

Dungu put his hand on Kerta's shoulder. 'You better get your friend back to Anjer. Quickly.'

Kerta nodded and got up from the dirt. He motioned to Jan and they moved away from the still-turning top.

'There are battles now,' the man shrieked. 'Against the Dutch. Men and women fighting with machetes against their rifles, cannons, gunships . . . That boat on this water here, *Berouw*, has been in my water, Aceh.'

Kerta jerked his head towards the man.

'And we fought. We fought those four heavy guns with rope across the river and oil-soaked *proas*. We couldn't stop it, but we tried. Like the fighters in the jungles in Bali. We remember your Prince Diponegoro . . .'

The men shouted and a drum began to beat as Kerta and Jan crept away from the beach and the village. They were not challenged, although Kerta thought the angry boy had seen them.

'What was this prince?' said Jan as they moved into the peace of Anjer.

Kerta shrugged. 'An old story, I guess.'

old battle

KERTA left Jan in the street of his house and walked back towards the lighthouse – but not along the Great Post Road, not near the men shouting on the beach. He turned from the sea at the Assistant Resident's house, the Dutch houses, towards the waterworks and its rope-bridge across the Anjer River. He moved through a cluster of trees to a bullock track through the paddies. The rice seedlings were only brushing the water, giving the village the impression of a dark ship sliding between the still sea and the gleaming paddies.

He could hear a few distant calls and a single laugh from the village, but that was all. He thought he could see a *proa* drifting from the beach, but it was too far away and the night was too dark. By the time he had wandered through the paddies and the jungle to Fourth Point his legs were beginning to wobble.

He thought that he should tell Jacob about the scene on the beach, but when he saw there were no lights at his bungalow he shuffled into his own hut. He mumbled to Ma – Pa was at the lighthouse – and slept near Dewi.

*   *   *

101

Ma nudged him next morning and sent him to Pa with breakfast – rice and sliced fish. Pa was sprawled against the gravel wall in the gallery and his eyes were ringed with blackness.

'Ma thought you'd like it up here instead of you climbing all the way down.' Kerta passed the wooden bowl to him.

Pa lifted his head slowly and took the bowl. 'Thanks. A good idea.'

Kerta was shocked by the exhaustion in Pa's eyes. 'I should have come earlier.'

Pa shrugged. 'Carver took over for a bit, and I think Krakatoa is quietening.'

Kerta looked at the distant island. It was still glowing and shunting smoke into the thick air.

'That tells you nothing, son. This tells you more.' Pa pointed his fork at the *proas* sailing away from the lighthouse. 'First there was a single *proa* from the next village – going by the sail I think it was Dungu – and then there was a fleet from the kampong. To make sure that Dungu doesn't get all the fish. Next the other villages will send *their* boats.'

Kerta frowned. 'I don't understand . . .'

Pa looked at him. 'Ma said that you saw some trouble last night.'

'There was a stranger trying to get the fishermen angry with the Dutch. Dungu got me to take Jan home . . .'

'Jacob says an Acehnese convict has escaped.'

'What was Diponegoro?'

Pa winced. 'You don't say that name in front of the Dutch. Jacob would throw us out of the lighthouse.'

Kerta sat down beside Pa and waited.

'Diponegoro almost drove the Dutch from Java.'

'A hero!'

'Yes, he was.'

'Pa, you sound like you want the Dutch out.' Kerta watched his face.

Pa hesitated. 'I guess everyone wants the foreign rulers to go home. The Indians, Vietnamese, Timorese, black Africans . . . My grandfather fought for Diponegoro. The Dutch did grim things a while ago. They made the Javanese farmers grow indigo for their blue clothes and a lot of people died of starvation, and they used slave labour to build the Grand Post Road. That road we walk to Anjer on, hundreds have died for.

'And then Prince Diponegoro started the revolt. The Dutch said that he was angry because the Grand Post Road would miss his area and he wasn't named as the next sultan of Yogyakarta. It didn't really matter what they said, though. Your great grandfather and thousands of other Javanese men followed him.

'His army thought that the prince was the *Ratu Adil* – the Just King. You know, Just King from the Javanese myths. And Diponegoro couldn't make a wrong move for the first few years. He fought a holy war against the Dutch army – and the Indian troops – winning battles all over Java. He ambushed troops, and set fires so the Dutch army couldn't find food or clean water in the jungle. The Dutch army was shrinking by a third every year so they brought troops from Europe, and Indian troops from outside Java. But it wasn't enough to stop the *Ratu Adil.*'

Pa stopped and watched a tramp steamer slide towards Krakatoa.

Kerta scratched his knee. 'But the Dutch are still here.'

'I keep on wondering; what if the Dutch had gone, if Diponegoro had won . . .'

Kerta looked at Pa. 'It would be great. No tramping soldiers, no smelly steamboats, no more fat, red-faced men telling us what to do . . .'

'No Jan.'

Kerta shrugged.

'No toffee.'

Kerta shrugged.

'No sitting in our high castle and looking down at the world going past us. No lighthouse. No Jacob.'

Kerta stared at the steamer and the *proas* and said nothing.

'It was the Dutch deal that finished Diponegoro. The Dutch gave back the land to the Javanese. My grandfather said he had to stop fighting when his old land was free for anyone. He said he had to grab it then.'

Pa pointed at the sailing *proas* drifting away from the kampong. 'Dungu just reminded the shouting crowd that they were fishermen and he was going to catch the best of the fish. Like the Dutch reminded my grandfather that he was a farmer.'

'But . . . what happened to the prince?'

'Diponegoro's army shrivelled like a cut lotus under the sun. He went to the Dutch general, De Kock, to talk about peace, but he was grabbed and exiled to Macassar. I think he died there.'

Kerta looked away and fumbled for words. 'Ah, Hasan said that you were a Dutch dog . . .'

Pa put the fork down. 'And maybe you too. Look, maybe the blacks in Africa, the Vietnamese, Timorese, Acehnese and even Javanese will show the front door to their foreign rulers, but not now. It is not the time. They are like mosquitoes – we can't get rid of them, but we can tolerate the bites. That convict is bad for us and the kampong. That's why Dungu pushed his proa out onto the water.'

Pa looked up at the smoking Krakatoa. 'Maybe I am a Dutch dog. Just polishing the panes, trimming the wicks, making sure the Dutch ships reach Batavia. Doesn't matter. Maybe I'm more like the convict than I think I am. After all, he is down in the kampong causing trouble for the Dutch because he has to. I'm here to save boats, because I have to – Javanese *proas*, American clippers, German warships, English steamboats – anything that scrapes the face of Antoe Laoet.

'After that terrible wave I *have* to.'

berouw

 THE next day Kerta come back to clean the panes while Pa fiddled with machinery. But by midday the sun was pushing through the floating ash and Kerta began to felt that his work on cleaning the panes was easing. The *proas* were now coming out from Pepper Bay, Anjer, the bays of Sumatra – everywhere – and there seemed to be more ships ploughing the strait now, ignoring the volcano. Some of them were actually deliberately sailing closer to get a good look.

In the early afternoon Pa called Kerta to finish. They met the Brothers as they climbed down. They were as cheerful as monkeys in a mango tree. Krakatoa? It was something to watch from the gallery, like ships. Their bright mood spread into Ma's lunch at the hut and when Kerta finished eating he asked Pa if he could see if Dungu had finished the top and he got a nod.

'A top?' Dewi squinted at Ma. 'Can I go?'

'With those tiny legs you wouldn't keep up.' Kerta pointed.

'I would too.'

'I don't think so, Dewi.' Ma shook her head with a smile.

'It's not fair! He goes everywhere!'

'You will when you grow a little bit,' Ma said.

Pa frowned.

'You'll do things that girls do,' Ma said quickly.

'I don't want to do things that girls do.'

'You are a girl,' said Pa gently.

'I don't care. The boys get all the fun. It's not fair.'

'Ah . . .' Pa touched his forehead. 'I forgot the trouble at the kampong. Maybe you better not go there.'

'But that was hours ago, another day . . .' said Kerta.

'All right, all right. Go.' Pa waved his hand at him. 'But be careful.'

Kerta moved quickly to the door, but he hesitated as he passed Dewi. 'Hey, look, when I get back, we'll try the top. Together.'

She looked at him and for a moment she flashed a bright smile, but then it began to wash away from her face. 'Promise . . .'

'Hey, I promise.' He waved at her and ran down the steps.

*   *   *

Kerta scowled most of the way to the kampong.

Dewi had treated his generous offer as if his promises were as useless as a goose honking. All right, he didn't play her jacks game, or her skipping, or go to her cooking party – but those were girl things. Well, if he was seen it would be murder . . .

But Kerta forgot about Dewi when he saw Dungu pulling his *proa* from the water without Hasan and hurried to help him.

'Thanks.' Dungu grunted as the boat slid easily across the dry sand. 'I've lost Hasan after my night sail. He hates me now and I could have used him today, but what can you do? Now, what does *this* boy want?'

Then he and Kerta heard a faint thumping in the water. Dungu glanced at the sea, shrugged and returned to business. 'Ah, is it fish, perhaps?'

'Well, there was . . .' Kerta looked over Dungu's shoulder at the Runner in the shadows of a beach hut. He was glaring.

'Well, you've picked a good time to come and join me. I have many fish, fish that I don't see often and some of them almost jumped into my boat. I managed to finish some very serious whittling out there but it was hard with those pushy fish . . . Um, what?'

'That man from Aceh who hates the Dutch is glaring at you.'

The thumping was increasing from the water, *tiching-tiching.*

Dungu glanced at him and shrugged. 'Don't worry about him. When I took my *proa* out yesterday the other fishermen who had been listening to him suddenly remembered that there were fish out there. Now that Krakatoa has finished he's lost his audience.'

He picked up a loaded basket of fish from the bottom of the boat and carried it to a big woman sitting on a bullock cart. 'Can you carry the other one, Kerta?'

The other one wasn't as large, but when Kerta pulled it from the boat he tottered around like an old sailor. Dungu had to put down his basket to rescue him.

Tiching-tiching . . .

'Another day with full baskets; you are emptying the strait!' the woman cried.

'I keep on telling you, I'm going to be rich.'

'You keep catching fish like that and I will marry you!' The woman flashed her betel-red teeth at him.

'Two wives! I'll work at it . . .'

'Dungu!' Kerta warned.

The Runner lurched from the shadow with his right arm behind him and moved towards Dungu.

'Come on, man. We don't do that here . . .' the woman called.

Tiching-tiching . . .

Dungu was moving away from the cart, looking at his *proa*. Kerta realised that his fishing knife was in the *proa* but the Runner was blocking his way to it. For a moment Kerta thought of sprinting towards the boat from an angle to get it. But he was too frightened. Dungu pulled his shirt off and wrapped it around his left hand.

'This is stupid,' the woman said.

The Runner shook his head and began to slide across the ground like a cobra.

'The *Berouw*!' the woman shrieked and rammed her arm forward.

The Runner looked back, stopped.

The gunboat slid, *tiching-tiching*, from a cluster of trees on the edge of the beach and churned into the kampong's shallow water. Men with rifles stood to attention in the bow and stern. The four heavy guns had swung towards the kampong.

'They are going to shoot us!' the woman shouted.

Several people slipped behind trees and huts but the Runner did not. The gunboat's paddles thrashed the water in reverse, until the ship was still. A small boy ran from the beach and a sailor swung his rifle to his shoulder.

The captain on the bridge wing roared. 'No!'

The sailor pulled down his rifle.

Kerta saw the Runner moving slightly towards some shadows.

Then there was a shout from the road. 'Soldiers!'

Hasan went to leap from the shadows but the Runner waved him back.

Several Indian troops were running from the Grand Post Road, fanning out through the trees and huts. The Runner skidded, turned and bolted around Dungu's boat, stumbled over the outrigger, but kept his feet and grabbed a coconut tree.

'Halt! Stay!' A Dutch officer with a red face pointed a pistol.

The Runner kept on running. The officer fired the pistol and a small piece of wood spun from the tree as the Runner swung away. The soldiers moved past the bullock, the cart, the woman, towards Dungu, lifting their rifles.

'Take him!' the officer shouted.

A soldier seized Dungu's arm.

Dungu looked at the soldier with a spark of alarm in his eyes. 'Kerta . . .'

'Not him!' the officer snarled. 'Him!' He fired again.

The Runner kept charging towards a rickety hut, but then he flapped his left arm and staggered a little.

'Run,' Dungu said quickly.

For an instant Kerta thought he was urging the Runner to keep on going, then he realised that Dungu meant *him*.

The soldier let go of Dungu's arm, looked at him, then swung his rifle up and jabbed the butt into his face. He raced after the Runner as Dungu collapsed like an old hut. Kerta swung away and sprinted past the bullock, past the spreading soldiers and the shouting officer. The officer's glinting gun was following his flight, and his back muscles tensed for the impact of the bullet. There was a single rifle shot.

'Who fired that? Do not fire,' shouted the officer.

Kerta stopped, looked back and saw that the *Berouw*'s sailor who almost shot the small boy was holding his rifle high. Dungu slowly lifted his head from the ground, but the Runner was lying still in the grass, now surrounded by the soldiers, and in the shadows Hasan was staring at his father in disbelief.

Jerking his head away, Kerta ran through the kampong as if there were ghosts on his shoulder. He stopped when he saw Jan standing in the middle of road. He pulled him to a tamarind tree.

'You shouldn't be here.'

'What happened?'

'The soldiers and the *Berouw* came after the convict . . .' Kerta looked at Jan and thought, He caused that. He told the army where the man was hiding. 'What are you here for?'

'You.' Jan nodded. 'I wasn't going through the kampong – especially when I saw the soldiers marching in – but I thought that maybe you could be coming to Anjer . . .'

There was some shouting and murmurs from the kampong and the road. The gunboat moving, *tiching-tiching*, towards Anjer as the officer marched his troops out of the kampong and across the bridge, as if he could hear a military band blasting away. In the middle of them was the Runner, hobbling with shackles round his legs and his shoulder stained with blood. He saw Kerta under the tamarind tree and glared.

Kerta thought, At least he is not dead. Yet. He turned to Jan. 'What did you want?'

'Do you want to go back to Krakatoa?'

the story

KERTA didn't tell Pa and Ma everything when he returned to the hut. He told them about *Berouw*, the soldiers, their rough treatment of Dungu, the shooting of the Runner and the marching him into Anjer. He did not tell them what Jan had asked. He was hoping that it would fade away, and it would have if Jacob hadn't dropped into the hut next morning.

'I assume that you heard about the hoo-hah in the kampong?' Jacob sipped his tea.

'Kerta was there,' Pa said.

'Really?' Jacob smiled at him. 'Seems that you are always there at the big event.'

Kerta was uncomfortable. 'I was only trying to get a top . . .'

Jacob laughed. So *Berouw* was aiming its guns at the man who had the top and you gave a touch of the sneezes to Krakatoa. I don't know, maybe I'd better tell Captain Lindemann that he could have trouble tomorrow.'

Pa and Ma looked at each other. 'Ah, why?' Pa said.

Jacob frowned. 'You don't know?'

113

Dewi looked up.

'I was going to tell you . . .' Kerta fumbled.

'Ah.' Jacob nodded. 'I had a word with the Master Telegrapher and *Loudon* is coming from Batavia with a load of Dutch adventurers who want to see Krakatoa. Professor MacDougal is one of them and he wants Kerta to come.'

'Oh,' Ma said flatly.

Jacob said, 'It might be very interesting.'

'Like hauling in a net of sharks,' Pa grunted.

Kerta began to smile. He was definitely not allowed to go.

Jacob talked with Pa and Ma about other things for ten minutes before he wandered over to the lighthouse. And then Pa and Ma turned to look at Krakatoa. Perboewatan's dark column was still there but now the smoke was drifting south, into the Indian Ocean, and the rest of the sky was blue with a few wisps of cloud.

'It looks better now,' Pa said. 'But I don't think so.'

'Kerta?'

'Yes.'

Kerta tried to hide the grin in face.

Ma looked again at Kerta as she talked very slowly. 'I don't know . . . I was thinking about my tiger.'

'The one you saw when you were six.'

'I didn't really see it, just a shadow, a rustle and a roar. But that was enough. I screamed out of the jungle and I wouldn't go back there. I still can't go into the jungle without shaking.'

'Ye-ss . . .'

114

'I wish Pa, Ma – anyone – had pushed me back into the jungle on a sunny day then. I would see that it's not all that bad and my shaking would go.'

Kerta's grin curdled as he realised what was happening.

'You think he should go?' Pa said.

'You said something on the gallery, something about seeing your demon.'

'Ah . . .'

'A shipload of Dutchmen and the Professor. How can be it dangerous?'

Pa sighed a little and turned to Kerta. 'Well, you can go. Unless you are a little afraid.'

For a split second Kerta was about to grab Pa's rescue line, but he saw Dewi's eyes locked on him. 'Scared? Never!'

* * *

Saturday, May 26

For most of Saturday Kerta counted down the minutes. Pa climbed the lighthouse with Carver as Ma went to the Anjer market and Kerta had the job of looking after Dewi. He took her to a rock under a coconut tree looking out to Krakatoa.

'What do you want to do?' He skipped a pebble over the water.

'Ma tells me stories . . .'

'I don't really know any.' He sat down and stared bleakly at the long column of smoke.

'Are you scared?'

'Me? That's stupid.'

'You *are* scared.'

Kerta rested his jaw on his knees and watched.

'I wouldn't be scared.'

'Yeah, you eat tigers for breakfast.'

'I do not!'

Kerta looked at Dewi. 'Stories you want . . . There's one that Ma probably didn't tell you.'

'Why?'

'Too scary.'

'I wouldn't be scared.'

'Are you sure?'

Dewi folded her arms.

'All right, there was a man called Adam –'

'Like the twin?'

'There are a huge number of Adams, but this one was a very important man, Nabi Adam. Up in the sky God liked him very much, so much a wicked angel was jealous, and stole Adam's seat. Because he couldn't sit there, Adam came down to the Earth. God was angry with the wicked angel and hurled him from Heaven to the Earth. The wicked angel blamed Adam for that and tracked him down, and told him, "I can't touch you, but all your grandchildren will fight each other for all time." That's why the Dutch always fight with the Acehnese, the Balinese and the Javanese, see?'

Dewi cocked her head. 'Um . . .'

'When the other angels heard what the wicked angel had done they muttered so fiercely that the people heard a big booming sound over their heads and called it "thunder". But there was one angel more furious than the others. He came down, saw the wicked angel and fired his fire tongue at him – people saw the fire tongue and called it "lightning". But the wicked angel danced past the fire tongues and battled the angry angel. The fight was causing terrible trouble – earthquakes, floods, fires, typhoons and volcanoes. Like that . . .' Kerta pointed at Krakatoa.

'The other angels tried to stop the fighting. They tried often; they built a coloured road from Heaven to Earth – the people called that "rainbow". But the wicked angel and the angry angel just kept fighting. The other angels wept at their failure – and the people called that "rain".

'God said this terrible fight will go on until the sun rises in the west and when the Earth stops turning. Then a terrible wind would pull every tree from the ground and all the seas on the Earth would be hurled from their deep beds. That will be called Doomsday.'

Dewi stared at the dull glow of Krakatoa for a while. 'You're making it up.'

'Make it up? No, no, I got it from Ma.'

She stared as his face for a long moment. 'I don't like it.'

Kerta turned from Dewi to the smoking volcano. 'Yes . . .'

loudon

 A FEW hours later, with a touch of sickness in his belly, Kerta watched the black steamer glide towards Anjer in the moonlight.

Harbourmaster van Leewen was making his Meerschaum pipe flair as he talked to Pilot de Vries at the Water Wharf. 'It is a waste of coal. For a Javanese boy!'

The Pilot shrugged and jumped onto his black steam launch. 'He is the son of Ndora, the lighthouse keeper. It makes a difference.'

The Harbourmaster snorted and walked away.

The Pilot shovelled more coal into the firebox as he saw Kerta approach and clanged the door closed. 'Right, lad, let it off.'

With a hurried charge Kerta whipped the ropes from the wharf's bollards, pushed the bow away from the wharf and leaped into the launch.

'Good lad, you'll be making Bas worry about his job.' The Pilot flashed his teeth.

Kerta smiled back and for a moment he forgot about Krakatoa. He could see the seams of the Pilot's face in the

118

light of the boat's swaying lantern, and remembered that he was a very, very old man. People said he took his teeth off to sleep and he had been seen walking around the church cemetery – probably picking his lot. He had been living around Anjer before the British arrived, maybe even before the French, and he had taught Bas how to run *Goliath*. But on his boat he wasn't old. He could take his launch to a wharf in a howling storm and tie it up perfectly by himself. He did not need Kerta.

But the Pilot had patted him, and that tasted sweet.

'Well, I don't envy your day,' the Pilot muttered.

And that jerked Kerta back to Krakatoa. 'Because of the volcano?'

'That is something I don't have to visit, but you have already, haven't you? But, no, it's the Batavia crowd I was meaning – a boatload of them! You can have that.'

Kerta looked at the ship as it drifted close and sucked his lip.

He had known that ship for a while. It was part of the Netherlands Steamship Company with a grand name, *Gouverneur-Generaal Loudon*, but it was a very normal steamboat with a single black-and-yellow funnel in the middle. Unlike the corvette *Elisabeth* there were no masts for sails, but there were high derricks and huge booms instead. Kerta had seen *Loudon* many times from the Fourth Point and Anjer and knew that the ship moved into shallow bays and the booms and derricks picked up and delivered goods to *proas* and barges. *Loudon* was a work-bullock; it could

119

pick up rubber and pepper as well as deliver mail, machinery, workers and convicts.

Kerta knew this ship, and he would have loved to sail on it, but not now.

Water churned at the stern, slowing the ship to a slow creep as the Pilot turned the launch towards its sea steps, the wooden ladder that snaked down the ship's side in calm water.

Kerta's throat was thick and he thought, It's coming back to me now. Everything, the fears on Rakata, shaking at Hasan's knife, running away from the attack on Dungu. He wanted to jump from this boat and swim away. Dewi was right. She was a tiny little thing, but she would face up to Orang Aljeh; he quivered at the smoke.

'Lad, catch the steps and help the man.' The Pilot eased the launch to the high wall of the *Loudon*.

Kerta moved across the boat, clutched one of the sea ladder's wooden steps, and waited without really seeing him for the single man to climb down from the ship's deck and help him into the launch. He was thinking, Mac won't be there. It's a bad joke by Jan. Maybe you can go back with the passenger and the Pilot.

'Kerta!' Mac was leaning on the ship's rail and waving.

Weakly he waved back, stepped from the launch to *Loudon* and watched the Pilot and the man putt towards Anjer.

Mac beamed at Kerta as he pulled himself to the deck, and slapped him on the shoulder. 'Jan's not coming?'

'No, his ma won't let him.' Lucky kid . . .

'Never mind, you're here. I told the volcano hunters

that you were there when the mountain erupted. That you live at Fourth Point, almost on top of Krakatoa. They want to talk to you.'

Kerta looked at Mac.

'It'll be all right. You will be fine. Krakatoa is finished, we're just going to say goodbye.'

Kerta said nothing.

'But now it's midnight and everyone is sleeping. I can get you a bunk in the crowded cabins, but you might prefer to be on the deck. Yes?'

Mac showed him to a coiled rope at the bow and walked to his hot, snoring cabin. Kerta sprawled on the rope and waited for the ship to start moving; he was sure that he wouldn't sleep tonight.

He stared at the stars through the derrick cables and thought of all the things that had happened in the last few hours: the Runner shouting, *Berouw*'s guns at the kampong, the shooting of the Runner, Jan with his deadly message . . .

Kerta could hear the gentle throbbing of the engine and felt the ship's pulse through his body.

But after a while he didn't.

*   *   *

Kerta woke to the sound of a heavy chain rattling across the deck and a massive splash. He jerked up and the early morning sun blasted his face.

'Hey, the kid is awake.'

'About time.' Footsteps came towards him and a shadow fell across his face.

Kerta opened his eyes to a man crouching over him. The man was European, but his face was lined and darkened by the sun. He had sideburns with flecks of white in the black. He tilted his black cap. 'I've been watching you from the bridge. You're from the Fourth Point?'

'Yes, Tuan Captain.' Kerta knew that *Loudon* was run by Captain Johan Lindemann, but he had not seen him until now.

'Do we throw him overboard for the fish?' A crewman with one gold earring was grinning down as he locked the chain on the winch.

'Not enough meat.' Captain Lindemann smiled. 'Maybe after breakfast, hey?'

Kerta twitched his lips a little. He wasn't quite sure about the two men.

'You are the lad who was on Krakatoa when the eruptions started? Well, look at it now . . .' The captain jerked his thumb towards the bow.

Kerta turned and stumbled to his feet in shock.

Krakatoa was less than two hundred metres from the bow of the *Loudon*. The ship wasn't moving now. It was anchored in the still water between Perboewatan, Verlaten and Polish Hat islands. Krakatoa looked like a kid's toy. Especially after what had happened there. The eastern Polish Hat was almost untouched by the eruption, with tall trees showing thick green foliage, but the wind had blown over the western Verlaten, covering trees and ground with grey ash.

Krakatoa had changed radically. Apart from a tuft of green on the edge of Rakata the island was barren. The purple flowers, palms, ferns, long grass, the jungle on the slopes, the pepper trees – the thick forest Kerta had walked through less than a week ago – were gone. The trees were now blackened skeletons or stumps, making the bare slopes look like a sheet in an unmade bed. Everything was covered by the grey ash, but around the Perboewatan crater there was black ash. There was no sound from the birds now, only the roar of the volcano as it hurled smoke and cinders into the air.

'Madmen,' said Captain Lindemann.

Kerta looked at him.

'A mob of Dutchmen want to climb that! I ask you, would you?'

Kerta shook his head very definitely.

'Exactly. Madmen.'

Suddenly the cabin doors swung open and a lot of excited Dutchmen ran towards the bow, pointing at the volcano and laughing. Some of them patted Kerta as they passed him.

Captain Lindemann shrugged at him and moved towards his bridge.

Kerta looked back at them crowding up on the rail and smiled.

He thought, Captain Lindemann will not put up with madmen – including Mac. This is where we stop. This is a big ship and it doesn't go any closer. That's all they are going to get.

Kerta saw Mac stretching near a cabin and joined him with a touch of smugness.

Breakfast was held under an old sail sling over the stern deck. Kerta ate with the rest of the travellers – coffee, bread with butter and jam – and tried to remember some of the names of the people that Mac introduced to him. It was a little hard – there were eighty-six travellers from Harmonie and Concordia clubs in Bavaria. Most of them were Dutch government and trade people, but there was a scattering of British and Germans.

Mac had become friends with Tuan Hamburg, a young man with a better camera than Mac's. While the others sipped coffee under the stretched sail Tuan Hamburg set his tripod against the rail and aimed his camera at the ballooning Perboewatan crater, capturing a rain of dark stones over the slopes.

Kerta learned quickly that the most important person among the passengers was *not* Mac but the Government Engineer Schuurman. Mac had told him that Tuan Schuurman had ordered *Loudon* to go to Krakatoa so he could study the volcano. The others – including Mac – were paying for Tuan Schuurman's trip. Tuan Schuurman actually talked to Kerta about how Krakatoa had been before, but as Kerta talked with him he wondered who was the most powerful on *Loudon* – Tuan Schuurman or Captain Lindemann. It could make the difference between men taking photos on deck and madmen wandering around the erupting volcano.

'Hey, we have company!' A man with a red bowler hat pointed.

A small grey steamship was moving slowly towards Verlaten Island, with the Dutch flag curling from its stern.

'What does she want?' The man with the red bowler hat and several others looked at Kerta.

Kerta groped. 'Um, it's the *Sumatra*, a navy ship. But I don't know what it's doing.'

'She is sounding the bottom around Krakatoa.' Captain Lindemann climbed down from the bridge and joined the breakfast. 'To see if the bottom has changed with these eruptions.'

Tuan Schuurman grunted. 'About time. I asked for that to be done days ago.'

Tuan Hamburg looked at him across the deck. 'Hey, Captain, why don't you move the boat closer?'

Captain Lindemann turned very slowly. '*Loudon* stays right here. This is close enough.'

'Oh, come on.'

He shook his head and sipped his coffee.

Kerta controlled his grin.

Tuan Schuurman lifted his head. 'That is not satisfactory.'

Captain Lindemann looked at him coolly. 'It is my ship.'

'I must go to that volcano. That is my job. I cannot see –'

'Yes.'

'– anything here. What?'

'Yes, I understand. You wish to study Perboewatan. So you will. I will give you one of the ship's boats.'

125

Kerta rocked back his head in alarm.

'Oh, that's fine.'

Kerta hunched a little as he watched Captain Lindemann order several crew to lower a lifeboat to the water. Tuan Schuurman shook the captain's hand before he climbed down the sea steps. Tuan Hamburg followed him with his tripod and camera, and was followed in turn by several members of the Harmonie and Concordia clubs.

Kerta gripped the rail and watched, laughing as they clambered down to the bobbing boat. Then he felt Mac's hand on his shoulder. He thought, He wants you to go to the island with everyone; what can you do? Accidentally fall from the sea steps?

'How do you feel, Kerta?' Mac murmured.

'I . . .' Kerta shrugged.

'Many of the travellers are going to stay on the ship. This is all – they don't want to get any closer to that volcano. Would you like to stay with them?'

Captain Lindemann was looking at Kerta with a curious lift of an eyebrow.

Kerta thought, I don't want to go with a boatload of madmen, Mac is letting me off. That's it. 'Yeah, well . . .'

'Don't worry about it, I'll tell you what it was like.' Mac wobbled his fingers at him and began to climb down.

Kerta flicked on a smile as he thought, That was it, and it was easy.

He took his hands off the rail, leant away – and stopped.

It's not. Pa will learn that I didn't go. Dewi will ask why – many times. Ma won't say anything, but she will know that I ran away from my tiger. And Hasan will know that those Dutchmen went to the volcano and I was too scared to go with them.

He clattered down the sea steps.

perboewatan

Kerta followed Mac without saying a word. Two *Loudon* crewmen were holding the boat against the bottom step, but none of the crew was in it. Instead Tuan Schuurman was at the rudder and men from the Harmonie and Concordia clubs were lifting the oars from the thwarts. Mac sat with Engineer Schuurman at the stern, but Kerta had to straddle the bow, as if he was a wobbling figurehead. There was no other space.

'Cast off,' Engineer Schuurman said, and the crewmen pushed off the boat. 'Hey, boy – Kerta, was it? – you keep your eyes open for rocks. All right?'

'Yes, Tuan.'

The clubmen swung the oars down and rowed quickly towards Perboewatan as the other travellers cheered from the ship's rail. And Kerta realised that there were only three people on the boat who were watching the volcano – Mac, Schuurman and him. The oarsmen were facing safe *Loudon* instead and he wished that he was rowing too.

As the lifeboat slid towards the volcano the roar seem to increase and fish darted wildly under the bow. Soon Kerta couldn't see the panicking fish because of the pumice. There were a few pieces around the anchored *Loudon,* but in the shallows of Perboewatan they were so thick on the water that the oars thudded almost every time they dipped. In the last metres the boat seemed to be set in concrete.

But Tuan Schuurman was ignoring the sea of rock and he was beginning to smile at the shivering crater. He then ordered the club oarsmen: 'Lay in Oars.'

The oarsmen stopped rowing and feathered the blades, dripping to the water. The boat was not yet at the beach but it would get there with inertia.

Kerta stared at the stained-black sand sliding towards him, and he knew he couldn't step on to that trembling earth. He would have to sit in the boat while the madmen climbed the volcano. Or better, he would jump from the boat and swim through the pumice to *Loudon* . . .

'Toss Oars.' The men swung the oars up to vertical and banged their oars' butts on the bottom of the boat.

But . . . any moment Tuan Schuurman will ask him to step down to hold the boat. And Mac will be expecting him to do that.

'Boat the Oars.' The men lowered the oars to the thwarts as Kerta felt the boat's keel grind into the sand.

'Kerta –' Tuan Schuurman didn't need the words.

Kerta leaped from the bow, splashed, took a step and held the boat as the men clambered down to the water. At least his back was to the volcano.

The oarsmen heaved the boat to dry sand. Tuan

Schuurman put small pieces of pumice in his bag, while Tuan Hamburg and Mac planted their tripods in the sand and shot the volcano. Then the men moved towards the crater. Mac packed away his camera and started following Tuan Hamburg, but he looked at Kerta and stopped.

'You're not going?' Mac said softly.

Kerta was leaning against the boat and staring at his right hand. It was trembling like a gasping fish. 'I . . . I can't.' He shook his head and turned away.

Mac glanced at the black smoke pouring from the crater. 'Yes, it's bad, when you see it up close. You want me to stay with you?'

Kerta jerked his head no.

'You're sure?'

'I'm all right.'

Mac walked from the beach, looked back for a moment, but then he began to climb after Tuan Hamburg.

Kerta felt the shimmer in the ground, saw pebbles dancing on the burned rock, and turned away to the motionless ship. He thought, It's worse than last time. Before, he didn't know if Orang Aljeh was sleeping or even dead, but now he *knew*. He could feel the movement under his feet.

He lifted his head. The ship was right there, safe in the water. He would be on that ship soon enough and those throbbing engines would get him away from here, back to Anjer. Back to the safe fortress of the lighthouse – *to Dewi*. And she would ask how it was, up there, where all the men were going.

Kerta turned again slowly. That horrible kid was worse than all the others. Pa would ask him how it was, but when he said that he didn't go up with the others then Ma would say what a good decision and Pa would nod. At least the boy put his foot onto his devil. Jan would think that he was a scaredy cat, but he would not say that to his face. Jan's lizard was always there. But Dewi would look at him with those brown eyes and frown a little bit and say slowly, 'Oh . . .' As if she had lost her hero brother.

He slowly frowned at the volcano, as if seeing it for the first time.

It was *not* worse than the first time. When he had climbed Rakata a few days earlier, Perboewatan had sounded like two armies were battling on the slopes, with heavy reports and cannon fire. Now there was just a steady roar. Eruptions of steam and rocks on the beach had chased the fishermen into the water, but now there were only tiny shivers. Then there had been tall water-spouts sliding around the island, but now the only things disturbing the water were nervous fish and hunks of pumice. Then there was black steam and ash shunting out from the crater . . . All right *that* was much the same. But the first time it had blocked the sun and coated the lighthouse glass. Now it was only spreading over the water.

Kerta pressed his lips together and pushed his body from the boat. He saw that the Dutch clubmen were beginning to swarm over the volcano. The man with the red bowler hat had sunk a leg to his calf in ash, but his friends laughed as they pulled him free; Tuan Hamburg was photographing Mac with several men, climbing a ridge; Tuan Schuurman was examining a black stump further up; one man was pitching pieces of pumice down to another man, who hit them with a walking stick; two men were racing to the crater. Orang Aljeh might have been ready to explode in fury, but the Dutchmen were not interested. Was it because they were invincible?

For a moment Kerta's legs did not move. His right foot would not move until he frowned at it. But then he was able to stride across the dark beach. He sprinted up a shallow ridge, kicking pumice down it as he went. Then he hurried past Tuan Hamburg and faltered.

'Ah, would you like me to carry something?' He pointed at the tripod.

'What? Oh.' Tuan Hamburg shook his head.

'You are sure? I am an expert with camera stuff.'

Tuan Hamburg smiled, but he kept his camera equipment to himself. Kerta shrugged and climbed quickly towards Mac. He took Mac's pack from his shoulder without saying anything.

'You've come.' Mac nodded. 'Good.'

They moved up a gentle slope towards the crater – Kerta surprised now by the smallness of Perboewatan. He knew the crater was only 120 metres tall, but now it seemed to be even less than *that*. The fires had left the volcano with nothing but thick ash and scattered blackened stumps, leaving the slopes looking like a Dutch seaman's stubble. Some of the men were moving very slowly past the stumps, as if they were singed animals looking for a place to die. Perboewatan was nothing more than absolute desolation, but somehow it didn't feel dangerous anymore.

But Mac stopped at a dip. 'I think *they* are pushing it.'

Two men were standing on the rim of the crater, silhouettes against the shunting of the clouds of smoke and ash. And then they gave a little dance on the edge.

'They are mad. Really.' Mac opened his camera.

They were joined by another three men, and others were moving towards the crater. Tuan Hamburg panted up to Mac and looked at his camera's view. 'You're not going up, then?'

Mac shook his head. 'It's a bit dangerous for me.'

Kerta looked at Mac and frowned. That didn't sound like him.

Tuan Hamburg shrugged. 'The whole island is perilous, but what can you do?' He grinned as he walked past Mac.

A minute later several men on a lower slope shouted in fear and pain. Kerta turned to see the men running and throwing up their arms to protect their heads. A high cloud of ash from the crater had drifted over the men, and was dropping hunks of pumice onto them. One man was hit on the shoulder, making him stumble for a few steps, but he recovered and ran with the others down the slope.

'See,' Tuan Hamburg called back. 'Dangerous anywhere.'

The running men finally stopped, but kept covering their heads with their hands while looking at the moving cloud. Kerta frowned at them and suddenly they looked funny, like clowns in a *wayang golek* shadow puppet play, and he almost laughed.

Tuan Schuurman walked past Mac, chipping at a piece of burnt wood. 'Silly lads,' he said. 'You have to get out of the way of the breeze, hey?'

Mac grunted and closed his camera.

Kerta tilted his head at Mac. 'You are really not going up to the crater?'

'This is enough.'

'It's not because of my chicken liver?'

Mac faltered for a moment. 'No, no, don't be daft.'

But Kerta had noticed the hesitation. 'Maybe –' He swallowed. 'Maybe we should go.'

'What?'

'Everyone is going up, even Tuan Schuurman.'

'They are a dumb lot.' Mac watched the engineer plodding towards the rim. 'I suppose we ought to see what they are seeing. I suppose.'

Mac sighed and began to climb. Kerta made a face and slowly moved up to the last section of the hill, always staring at the men on the crater. As he moved closer the men seemed be etched against the black eruption and some of them had a soft glow on the edges of their legs.

'Be careful,' Tuan Schuurman called.

A man turned to him and Kerta froze in a half step. The man's face was lit with a flaming light, as if he was ablaze. He waved his hand at Kerta and turned back to the crater.

134

It's all right, Kerta thought. It's only the light.

His foot crunched down on a pumice rock as they climbed on. The roar from the eruption was now pounding in Kerta's ears with such intensity that he opened his mouth like a stunned fish. The boiling black smoke shifted to reveal a red glow at the edge of the crater and the air was heavy with the foul smell of sulphur and charred rock.

He wanted to stop, to run down the dead slope, but his feet stumbled on as if they were in charge. Mac shouted at him but he couldn't understand his words. Kerta shook his head. Mac nodded and kept going until he reached the other men.

Kerta plodded up to him, stopped, then slowly his legs began tremble. Mac patted his hand on his shoulder, but Kerta didn't notice. He was at the lip of the crater, his feet were enduring the heat of the ash through his soles, but he couldn't feel it. He could only stare down.

The crater was almost one kilometre across, but its bottom – only 200 metres down – was as narrow as 30 metres. He could run up and down that easy slope to the end, if there wasn't anything there. But there was. Steam was hissing from crevasses and crumbling fissures inside the crater, while smoke and ash were coiled in the heart of the pit. Everything – the ridges, the steam, the tumbling ash – glowed a throbbing dark red. There were stones rattling around the lower slopes as if trying to burst out of the crater. He could hear crackling and sharp reports. The walls sounded like they were about to collapse in a roar into the pit.

'It's like a party! Like champagne corks popping!' A man shouted close.

Kerta flicked his eyes sideways and was amazed to see the man with the red bowler hat and three men *inside* the crater. They were standing on a ridge ten metres below the lip.

'Now, that *is* madness,' Mac said.

Kerta looked beyond the four men into the glowing smoke, into the pit, at the white-hot lava slithering from the ground. He could feel the volcano shaking through his feet.

Tuan Schuurman pointed down to the pit and boomed, 'We've found the portal of Hell!'

The Harmonie and Concordia men stood quietly on the rim of the crater for a long moment.

Kerta stared, and he thought, Down there is Orang Aljeh. I can see him.

He shivered and Mac felt it.

Mac took his hand from Kerta's shoulder, bent down and looked at his face. 'All right?'

'I'm all right.' And then Kerta blinked. I am all right. Really. I am looking down at the face of Orang Aljeh and it's hideous, awful, but that's it . . .

The man with the red bowler was creeping towards the billowing smoke as Tuan Hamburg tossed a hunk of pumice down the throat of the volcano. Some men laughed and copied him. Kerta picked up a warm rock and then hefted it several times, as if trying to judge its weight.

'Careful . . .' Tuan Schuurman warned the man with the red bowler as he capered at the edge of a ridge.

'I'm going to put the Devil's fire out!' He groped with his trousers and men roared in laughter as they saw that he was doing.

Mac said to Kerta, 'We shouldn't be here too long. It is an active volcano. Are you ready to leave?'

Kerta turned and saw the small warship *Sumatra* pushing slowly through smoke, ignoring the falling stones. Nobody was troubled by Orang Aljeh this day.

He nodded at Mac and then as he moved away from the rim he hurled his rock into the crater.

hasan

 WHILE Kerta and Mac were walking towards the beach *Loudon* blasted its steam whistle. Against the roar of the volcano the whistle was a feeble peep across the still water, but they could hear it. It blew several times as Kerta and Mac approached the beached boat, and the men reluctantly peeled off from the crater and came down the slopes.

Tuan Schuurman hurried past in annoyance. 'Listen to him! We were coming, but he nags us like an old washing woman.'

'It's all right,' said Mac. 'He's worried about us.'

Tuan Schuurman snorted. 'Captain Lindemann is only worried about his lovely *Gouverneur-Generaal Loudon*. We know what this volcano is doing – we did look down the throat of it – while he listens to the rumbles two kilometres away.'

The hooting stopped once the boat was pushed from the beach. Kerta looked over his shoulder to the volcano, but then he turned to *Loudon*. He had seen it all.

After they reached the ship, he clambered up the sea steps behind the laughing men, watched the crewmen hoisting the

138

boat from the water and pulling up the anchor, and felt the engine stirring under his feet. Captain Lindemann was in a hurry to leave Krakatoa. Which was all right for the club men and Kerta, but Mac and Tuan Hamburg would have been happier with another hour there.

As *Loudon* moved away the sun sank behind Verlaten Island and shadows crept across Krakatoa's black hills. The red glow of the crater of Perboewatan and the tint in the ash clouds intensified and the still water caught the fire.

'That is beautiful,' said Tuan Hamburg, and took his last photo of Krakatoa.

'Yes, it is,' Mac said softly with a touch of surprise.

'Will you be coming back?'

Kerta looked at Mac and was disappointed when he shook his head.

'I think it's finishing now.' Mac glanced at the pumice in his hand. 'So it's over for me; I'll have to see a volcano in Hawaii.'

'Oh.' Kerta looked at the receding Krakatoa for a long while from the deck and he finally decided that he wouldn't bother to go back without Mac. He had seen the teeth of Orang Aljeh, and after that there was nothing left to see.

*　　*　　*

The *Loudon* steamed towards Anjer as the stars took over the sky, but the ship didn't stop there. Captain Lindemann slowed the engine near Anjer so Kerta could catch a cruising fishing *proa*.

Mac shook Kerta's hand at the rail, 'Take it easy.' He stopped and frowned. 'I'd wish to come back here, Kerta. But that would be a curse to Anjer. Krakatoa would have to call me back and you can't want that. So . . .' He stepped back with a sad smile.

Kerta climbed down the sea steps, then looked back at Mac and saw the captain behind him on the wing bridge touching his cap with a finger. He waved at both of them and swung into the *proa* as *Loudon* moved slowly towards Thwart-the-Way, towards Batavia.

* * *

The *proa* passed under the lifted drawbridge and dropped Kerta on the steps of the fort. He hurried into the abandoned buildings, hoping to catch Dungu in the kampong on the way home. Now he could think about the top . . .

'Whiteskin.'

He stopped and turned around. The moon was picking out the boy, Hasan, standing on top of a cannon near the mud parapet.

'Yes, you . . .' Hasan pointed.

Kerta thought of striding quickly away, but that felt wrong. Instead he walked towards him.

Hasan had dropped astride the cannon, ready to run after Kerta, but he was now uncertain. 'I saw you creeping from that Dutch ship.'

Kerta shrugged.

Hasan pointed at a pyramid of iron cannonballs below him. 'I wanted to fire those and sink your ship.'

'Why? There were no Dutch soldiers on that ship.'

'Doesn't matter. It's a Dutch ship full of whiteys. I aimed this thing at *Berouw* many times. It sinks every time it passes here.'

'So why didn't you?'

'No gunpowder . . .'

'Ah.'

'Your prince should have taken this fort and stopped the ships getting to Batavia. Everyone knows how good this fort could be. My pa said the French were here and the British were here as well as the Dutch.'

Hasan slid from the cannon. 'The prince should have been here. So I have taken it.'

'Fine.' Kerta looked around. The telegraph cable was still connected to the block-house but the two bunkhouses were sagging ruins and the mud parapet around them had slowly washed away. There had once been a ditch following the parapet to the canal, but there were only a few puddles left. The soldiers had marched from the fort two years ago to another town, leaving only the telegraph cable and the old cannons. 'You can have it.'

'It's better than living in a Dutch lighthouse.'

Kerta said nothing.

Hasan tightened his mouth. 'You know where my pa is now?'

'I don't know.'

'He is breaking rocks on the road to Batavia. In chains.'

'I am sorry.'

'Sorry!' Hasan leaped from the cannon to face him. 'You told the bloody police.'

'I did not.'

'You are a liar.'

'I am not a liar.'

Hasan shoved his face close to Kerta. 'Yes?'

Kerta said nothing and looked into his eyes.

Hasan's eyes shifted slightly. He took a step back. 'Someone told the police.'

Kerta nodded.

'It must have been your greasy Dutch friend.'

Kerta did not say anything.

'That's the same as you telling the police.'

'It's not.'

Hasan looked at Kerta and a faint frown drifted across his face. 'Yes, well . . .'

Kerta stepped away and began to walk out of the still fort. Then he turned. 'I'm sorry about your pa.'

Hasan lifted his head sharply. '*Berouw* shot him like a dog and chained him. Because he wanted the Javanese to join Aceh in the fight. And maybe they will one day.'

Kerta remembered how Pa had said it may happen but not yet. As he moved away he said, 'Maybe.'

'Hey!'

Kerta looked back and Hasan was pointing towards the glow of Krakatoa.

'Did you go there?'

He nodded.

'All the way?'

He nodded and walked away.

Hasan called after him, 'One day.'

*   *   *

Kerta passed the British monument and the small mosque to the Great Post Road, wandering past the clattering of the market, thinking of Hasan and his father. He was trying to put to *his* pa in the sandals of Hasan's pa.

But it was hard; both fathers had a deep anger – for the Dutch or for Orang Aljeh – but that was it. But, but, yes, Pa cheered when Dungu's *proa* stopped the Runner's rebellion, but Pa would *not* tell the police where he was. Maybe Pa felt that *he* could have been the Runner another time? And how would *he* like to be Hasan?

'Kerta!'

Jan waved from the edge of the noisy market. He was standing with a group of Dutch youths. Kerta lifted his hand, but then he looked back at the darkened fort.

'You know where *he* has been?' Jan said to the youths, pointing. He began to stride across the road.

But Kerta dropped his hand and looked away from Jan.

Jan stopped in the middle of the road in confusion and watched quickly as Kerta walked away.

dewi

DUNGU waved at Kerta from his hut and patted a rag. Kerta joined him with a weak smile.

'It is finished.' Dungu took the rag away and placed the top in his hands and draped a thin cord over his shoulder.

Kerta nodded.

'What's the matter?'

'Nothing . . . I'm – I saw Hasan, and –'

'Poor kid. Where is he?'

'The old fort.'

'And he had a go at you.'

'Not really. He wants to sink *Berouw* with one of the fort's cannons.'

'I'll try to get to get him back in the *proa*. But this is a bit easier.' Dungu flicked the rag away and passed the top to Kerta.

Kerta felt the weight and twitched a faint smile. 'Yes, it is. Thank you.'

'Try it tomorrow morning, all right?'

'First thing,' he promised as he moved towards the road.

'Hey,' Dungu gestured at the red glow with his thumb. 'You didn't do that, did you?'

Kerta grinned back. 'I spoke to the old Orang and he promised he would quiet down.'

*   *   *

Ma saw Kerta faintly in the shadows of the track and hurried to him. She threw her arms around him, then pushed herself from him and stared into his face.

'Are you all right?'

'Oh, yes, better than that, I saw –'

'Good, good. Now . . .' Ma's eyes hardened.

'Is there something wrong?'

'Dewi was shaking last night.'

'Oh.'

'She had a very bad nightmare about the angels fighting and the end of the world.'

'Oh.'

'Yes, oh. What's wrong with you? Dewi is a little girl. You have to begin to realise how your funny games may affect people badly. You have to think before you open your mouth.'

Kerta lowered his head. 'Sorry.'

'All right. Pa doesn't know about it. We'll drop it.'

They walked to the hut.

*   *   *

145

When Dewi made a face at him he lifted her hands and put the top into them.

'You got it . . .' She stared in awe. 'It's very heavy.'

'It's going to be ours.' Kerta glanced at Ma. 'We're going to make it fly tomorrow.'

'Fly?' Dewi's hands sagged with the top.

'Fly. It will.'

'How was it?' Pa said.

'It was great.'

'Nothing wrong at all?'

'Nothing at all.'

'Ma was worried about you all day – until she saw the *Loudon* came back.'

Ma snorted as she put a plate of fish and rice before Kerta. 'But you're here. So it's over.'

'Did you really get onto the volcano?' Dewi looked up at her hero brother with wide eyes.

'Walked everywhere. Even to the crater.'

Ma jerked her head up. 'What?'

'Everyone was up there. Mac – Tuan Mac, and the Engineer from Bavaria, and the cameraman – everyone.'

'I thought you would see it from the ship! That was stupid – all of them! What happens if the volcano had erupted then?'

'Well, it didn't.'

'You are very lucky! The Dutch – I think the whole white people are stupid anyway – but I didn't think that you would catch their idiocy.'

146

'Well, he's here.' Pa shrugged. 'It's all right.'

'He is not going out there again. That is that.' Ma glared at Kerta.

Kerta nodded. He didn't need to see it again.

Pa cocked his head and looked at Kerta. 'What did you see up there?'

Kerta smiled at his father. 'I saw the Orang there.'

'How?'

'There was a crack in the bottom of crater. Through the smoke I could see a red hot fire.'

'The eye.'

'Yes.'

'I wish . . .' Pa sighed softly. 'I wish that I'd seen the Antoe Laoet. I only saw a bump in the sea.'

*　　*　　*

Next morning Kerta and Dewi climbed down from the hut with the top. Dewi was carrying the cord with both hands raised, as if she was presenting a gift to a sultan. Kerta found some dry, level ground and pulled out a seagull feather. Jacob's boys swung from the railing of their bungalow as they watched.

'Is that what makes the top fly?' Dewi said with wide eyes.

Kerta turned the feather in his hand, looked at her and shrugged. 'Sort of.' And swept the ground with the feather.

'Does that make magic?'

'Here, everything is magic.'

Adam and Dirck ran across. 'What are you doing?' said Dirck.

'Magic,' Dewi said, then turned to Kerta. 'I can do it, can't I?'

Kerta passed the feather and watched Dewi dancing around the ground. Then he wrapped the cord around the top, gripped the end of it and stepped back. Dewi and the twins squatted and waited.

He hurled his arm at the ground, released the top and whipped his arm back as Dungu had done. The top hissed in the air, bounced on the hard ground, wobbled, the edge touched the ground and then it skittered along the causeway.

'It's not working,' Adam said in disappointment.

Dewi collected the top and brought it back. 'Is it hard to do?'

Kerta grunted.

The next few attempts were much the same – skidding on dry mud, shimmying sideways, and even bouncing down the rocks. But then Kerta did everything right – the top wobbled for a moment, then it steadied and softly whistled.

Dewi stumbled back with her eyes wide. 'It is alive!'

Kerta's head jerked slightly in surprise, but then he realised what Dungu had done. There was a small piece of bamboo fixed to the top and as it spun it whistled softly. 'It's all right; it's supposed to do that. Now it's flying.'

'Is that it?' Adam said.

'Magic? That's nothing.' Dirck snorted and walked back to the bungalow.

'Um, it doesn't fly very high, does it?' Adam followed his brother.

Dewi lowered her head to the ground and squinted at the bottom of top. 'What does it do now?'

'Nothing much, really,' Kerta admitted.

'What do we do?'

'We just watch, see how long it can spin.'

She watched the pattern of the top blur until she wrinkled her nose. 'It is not as fun as knuckles.'

'Sorry.'

She looked at him and frowned. He had never said 'sorry' to her before. She suddenly moved around the top, squatted beside him and linked her arm with his. 'But you made it go.'

'Yeah.'

'How long will it last?'

'I don't know.' He shifted his eyes to the distant volcano.

Dewi saw the movement. 'I wouldn't like to go there. Was it scary?'

'Ah, that was nothing . . .' Then he looked at her face. 'Yes, it was frightening. I didn't want to get off the ship.'

'But you did. Was it as bad as the fire from the mouth of the good angel?'

Kerta looked at Dewi.

'He was fighting the bad angel,' said Dewi.

Kerta hesitated but nodded. 'Something like that, spe-cially down the crater. But the volcano will stop soon.'

'No, it can't!' She shook her head.

'What's wrong?'

'If they stop fighting, the world stops.'

Kerta closed his eyes. 'Hey, Dewi, it's only a story.'

'A story . . .'

'Like Ma's story about the monkey who got a crocodile to carry him across a river.'

'A story.' Dewi stared at the red glow of Krakatoa and said nothing.

the offer

MASTER Telegraph Schruit strode out of the lighthouse track with a black bag on his shoulder. He passed Kerta whipping his top as a bored Dewi and the twins lay about in the grass watching, he waved at Ma as she swept the steps and then marched to Jacob's bungalow. Jacob, sprawling on a cane chair on the veranda, looked up from his newspaper.

'What's up?'

'I want to borrow your lighthouse.'

Jacob waved his walking stick at Fourth Point. 'Take it away.'

'Thank you.' The Master Telegrapher lowered his load carefully and took the black bag from Lloyd's Agent Schu-it's gleaming telescope.

'Ah, you want to go up to the gallery and see Krakatoa. Kerta!' Jacob waved.

'Professor MacDougal hasn't really left us. He's been swapping telegrams from Hawaii with Engineer Schuurman and they are worried about the pieces of pumice they took from the crater. The pieces are from deep magma – unusually deep. So they want me to tell them what Krakatoa is doing. That's why I've got Schuit's telescope and he's using Pilot de Vries's.'

'I don't know whether you can see anything now.'

'Doesn't matter, really. Just so long as they don't ask me to go there. We've only got one Krakatoa climber here and it's not me.'

Kerta picked up the telescope with a slight hunch.

'But I am glad that Kerta is here. There is a job for him . . .' The Master Telegrapher laughed at Kerta's wince. 'Nowhere near Krakatoa. Talk about it later.'

Jacob cocked his eyebrows at Kerta with a light smile.

The Master Telegrapher was about to walk towards the lighthouse when he glanced at Jacob's folded *Amsterdamse Courant*. 'Oh, yes, news. We have a little news in sleepy Anjer. Someone broke into Li Yang's shop last night.'

'Really? What was taken?'

'That's what was odd. Nothing. The thief broke the lock and moved things, but he did not take a thing. Li Yang says that he is caught in a terrible bind – he is very happy that he wasn't robbed, but he feels that his shop is full of marvellous things and he has been insulted by the thief.'

'Very odd.'

*   *   *

The Master Telegrapher rested the telescope on the gallery rail, looked at Krakatoa and sighed. He didn't see Krakatoa.

152

He saw a grey haze on the water and a thin curl of smoke wandering into the sky. 'I did hope that it would better here than Anjer. Is it always like this?'

'Almost.' Kerta was looking down at Adam wrapping the cord around the top as Dewi played with pebbles. He felt slightly sad.

'Never mind, let's talk.'

Kerta turned, his eyes troubled.

'That volcano is causing no end of bother,' Schruit said. 'Everyone wants to send a telegraph to Anjer these days.'

Kerta nodded very slowly.

'I need a bright lad to deliver telegrams around Anjer.'

He couldn't quite understand.

'Kerta, would you like the job?'

'Me?' He blinked. For a moment he thought of Hasan's anger against Dutch licking dogs, but then he began to beam. 'A real telegrapher?'

'I'll talk with your father. There is some money . . .'

messenger

Pa was happy to see Kerta working as a Telegram Boy and Ma was delighted – maybe because he would stop hanging around the hut – but Dewi was a little peeved.

'The twins will push me around now,' she said.

'But you always push *them* around,' Ma said.

Dewi thought a bit then ran to bully the twins.

Kerta went to the telegraph office and he was inducted as a Telegram Boy. Telegrapher Berg, a bony man with a thin moustache, jammed a long Dutch peaked cap on his head. 'That's all we had,' said Master Telegrapher Schruit as he put a cotton bag on Kerta's shoulder and made him promise that he would deliver all the telegrams and never read them. And then Telegrapher Berg slipped an envelope into the bag and pushed him through the door.

As Krakatoa simmered Kerta began to carry the telegrams across Anjer, from the Assistant Resident's shining glass house, to Li Yang's, to the fishmonger in the market. Most of the messages were good news and he was welcome; one of them was actually for him; but one was troubling and the first one started things badly.

Harbourmaster van Leewen glared at Kerta and the envelope in his hand. 'What's that? A telegraph from a monkey! You stole it, didn't you?' Finally he snatched the message from Kerta, muttering, 'Probably it's someone else's and it's been lost for a week . . .'

But the next one was Doctor Dillié and he was marvellous. 'You have become Anjer's Telegram Boy? Congratulations, lad! Now I can relax, knowing that my contacts will get through.'

He insisted that Kerta have a glass of his special lemonade to celebrate. The doctor was from France, not Holland, and his garden were scented with spices, odd vegetables and fruit. He spiked his lemonade with spices.

Kerta learned about the messages from the people who received them . . .

The fishmonger was slitting up a fish in her open shop in the market when he arrived. 'A telegram? For me? That is terrible news! Don't stand there, boy, open it!' She waved the knife and the fish at him. He hastily ripped the envelope and she grabbed the message from his fingers. 'Kalimbang? Oh, oh! My little sister has a baby! A boy! About time!' She was surrounded by a crowd from the market, people slapped her on the back and she shoved the fish into Kerta's bag. For the rest of the day Kerta had to apologise for the smell of his messages.

When Kerta was walking along the Waterfront he saw Li Yang cleaning up his big bronze lock and talking to his wooden Indian. 'See, this has stopped the thieves. You don't frighten anyone.' The wooden Indian glared. Li Yang took the message with a sigh. 'That is family. I get them all the time. This time the Sydney family wants me to take their third dumb son to learn the business. My business. I think I'll tell them we have volcano trouble . . .'

Tuan Baha in his coffee shop snatched his message from Kerta. 'I don't believe it. It's my third son in Nebraska. Last time I saw him he was working with horses on the Tigris River, not far from my old Baghdad home. But now? You'd never guess what he's doing. Well, he's gone off with the barbarians in America. He's had it with chasing cows and now he's looking after horses in something called "Buffalo Bill's Wild West Show". Maybe I should buy Li Yang's wooden Indian . . .'

After a while, sometimes Telegrapher Berg told Kerta what the message said. Like the one from an army captain who wanted to map Krakatoa and wanted to know if Assistant Resident Thomas Buijs could join him.

When Kerta arrived at the house of the Assistant Resident, Tuan Buijs was supervising the planting of flower bushes as his wife and two children were playing with a big red ball on the grass. 'Good, good,' were his words as he took the message, but he was looking at the flowers instead of the message. 'What do you think, boy? The yellows first or the red . . .' Then he read the message and looked at Kerta. 'You've been there, Krakatoa. Is it safe?'

Kerta's eyes widened. *He wants me to go there!* 'Ah, safe . . .'

156

'Nobody died, did they?' Then he looked at his squealing daughters. 'I'll think about it.'

And then one day Telegrapher Berg passed a message to him without saying anything and suddenly Master Telegrapher Schruit looked like a furtive monkey. Kerta started to move for the door, glancing at the address, and stopped. 'Kerta Ndora . . . That's me!'

'Really, well you better open it,' said Schruit.

'It's Mac!' Kerta squealed and read, *Congratulations Telegraph Boy Hawaii too quiet will come back to Krakatoa will bring you a velocipede.* 'What is a velocipede?'

'It sounds like a monster,' said Berg.

'I haven't the faintest,' said Schruit.

*　　*　　*

At the end of a Friday afternoon Master Telegrapher Schruit presented the Telegram Boy with some worn coins. Kerta strolled through Anjer and the kampong, clinking them in his pocket as he wondered what he would do with them. He passed a muddy, grinning Hasan, but he didn't wonder about that for a second.

The following day, he was still thinking about the coins when he went with Ma and Dewi to the market. But then he had a sudden glimmer. 'Ma, can I take Dewi to Li Yang?'

'Oh, yes, yes, can we?' Dewi beamed.

'All right, all right. Here in half an hour.'

Dewi had been to Li Yang's before with Ma, seen its

shelves of tea, hats, shovels, candles, treacle – sometimes even fireworks – and bright toys and sweets. She would stare at the full glass bowls while Ma bought the tea and then they would go, leaving the sweets in their bowls. But today was different – her brother was clinking as he walked.

They walked past the wooden Indian and through the door.

Li Yang beamed at them from his counter, which could be a little terrifying. His teeth glinted with gold and his face cracked like the wooden Indian's, but even Dewi had got used to him. 'Good Tuan Kerta, and beautiful Dewi, isn't it a lovely day?'

Kerta shook his pocket. 'I have money now.'

'Ah, yes. Then what can I do for you? Sweets?'

'I suppose.' He placed two small coins with holes on the counter.

'You are in among the rich! Two five-cents! Any of those.' Li Yang waved at the glass bowls and rows of wrapped toffees.

'Um . . .' Kerta looked across at Dewi. 'What do you think?'

Dewi was staring at a stitched Dutch doll, with bonnet, blue dress, white apron and plaited blonde hair. 'What?'

'You pick.'

'Oh.' Still locked on the doll, Dewi was confused. She was in the shop because her brother had some money and she was interested to see what he might buy, and maybe she would be given a single sweet, but that was it.

'Well, liquorices, fudge, caramels, toffees . . .'

Dewi dragged her eyes reluctantly to the glass bowls. 'Um, maybe . . .'

'Wait a bit.' Li Yang had seen Dewi's look. He walked quickly to a box behind the counter, pulled something from it and dusted it behind his back. 'I think Dewi wants a doll, yes?'

Dewi watched Li Yang with huge eyes.

'Now the others there are a little expensive. And they are little Dutch girls. However I have this . . .' He showed a small doll, still dusty. The dark hair, the eyes, nose and the crooked mouth were drawn on the light cream head. She had a brown skirt and her arms and legs were elongated and thick.

'That's me!' Dewi reached up and took the doll from Li Yang very carefully, then she whipped her head to Kerta. 'Can I, please?'

Kerta winced, but he remembered that Dewi couldn't spin the top and there were the nightmares that he had given her. He looked at Li Yang. 'Um, how much would it cost?'

Li Yang smiled at him and slid one of the five-cent coins towards him. 'Now you can use the other coin to get your sweets. All right?'

Dewi wandered out of Li Yang's, talking to the doll she was cradling. Kerta trailed after her with a small brown paper bag and a huge grin.

*   *   *

Telegrapher Berg didn't tell Kerta what the message to Tuan Joost was. 'Better not.' But he didn't really want to know. He just hoped that Jan wasn't at home.

But he was. He swung the door open and his face became cold. 'So?'

Kerta touched the long peak of his cap and lifted the envelope. 'Ah, I have something for Tuan Joost.'

'He's not here. He's at his depot.'

'Oh.' Kerta turned away.

Jan sighed. 'I can take it.'

Kerta hesitated.

Jan snatched the envelope from him, opened it and squinted at him. 'Did you see this, Telegram Boy?'

'No.'

'No? Doesn't matter. It's just about a shipment of gunpowder.'

'Oh.'

'For blowing up tree roots and for Li Yang's son to make his fireworks . . .'

'I know.' Kerta turned away, stopped and turned back. 'Look, that time outside the market . . . It was only that Hasan was watching.'

'I understand. You are Javanese and I am Dutch, and that's everything.'

Kerta walked heavily away.

the party

 Dewi stomped with her doll down the
steps of the hut. 'I should go to the party.
It's not fair. Upya thinks so.' The doll nodded.

Ma took her hand and walked with Pa and Kerta towards
Jacob's bungalow. 'You wouldn't like it, Dewi. A lot of very
old people just talking.'

'He's going!' She pointed with the arm of her doll at
Kerta.

'I don't want to go,' muttered Kerta. He was carrying
his top.

'He has to. They all are talking about the volcano. They
have an army captain who went there just a few days ago
and Kerta has been there.'

'Twice,' Pa said with a smile.

'It's going to be terrible . . .' Kerta promised.

Dewi looked up at the bungalow and saw Jacob walking
down with a smile. Rara, Jacob's amah, was giving a drink to
Carver on the veranda, with Dirck and Adam making faces
at Dewi. 'This will be worse.'

'Are you frightened of the twins?' Pa said.

161

'Frightened of *them*?' Dewi shook her hand from Ma's, grabbed the top from Kerta, ran past Jacob, galloped up the steps of the bungalow, shoved the top into Adam's hand and pushed Dirck.

Jacob laughed as he joined Ma and Pa. 'Just as well we've got twins to protect each other.'

Adam raised the top, to thank Kerta. He had mastered the top, but Dirck wasn't interested and Dewi had Upya.

Jacob looked at Kerta as he led him from the bungalow. 'Why the misery face? It won't be so bad.'

But Kerta caught a murmur from Ma.

'But it will.'

*　*　*

Kerta thought about Ma's mumble all the way to the Great Post Road, through the kampong, across the stone bridge, into the scented Dutch Quarter, to the front gate of the Joost family house. And it was there that he began to work it out.

He was worrying about things as walked towards the gate, like he didn't want to go to the party because people would ask him awkward questions about Krakatoa – especially this army captain – and probably he wouldn't know the answers. He knew Orang Aljeh, but the Dutch didn't want to know about ghosts and that was all he knew. Maybe Ma understood that, but she wouldn't know about the other thing.

That he didn't want to face Jan. After that moment at

the Joost house he would rather fight Hasan or sniff Orang Aljeh.

And then Ma stopped at the gate of the Joost house.

Jacob smiled at her and pushed the gate open.

Ma remained outside in the street.

Kerta looked at his mother, saw her lips pushing at each other, saw her hands were clenching.

In that moment he realised that Ma was not worried about him – she was worried about *herself*.

'Are you all right, love?' Pa said.

Ma stiffened a little, nodded and stepped into Tuan Joost's bright flower garden.

Kerta knew what was happening. Ma was about to walk into a gathering of wealthy Dutch women with polished necklaces, dresses which creaked as they moved, and she wore a bracelet made from the bone of a squid, a gift from Carver. She was expecting to be sneered at the moment she walked into the house. But Pa was almost as vital as Jacob in the Fourth Point lighthouse. He knew how important he was, so he wasn't feeling Ma's fear.

It didn't matter. On the doorstep plump Mrs Joost squeezed Ma to herself as if she was a lost sister, bustling her towards Dutch women in the crowded lounge.

Madam Schuit who ran the hotel asked, 'One thing I've been wanting to know; how do you manage a mob of men jammed into a lighthouse?'

Ma laughed. 'Simple. I let my daughter, Dewi, push them around . . .'

Then Kerta saw the wife of Li Yang drifting towards Ma and behind her there was her husband, with the Imam, Baha, and his wife talking to the Assistant Resident Thomas Buijs. There was the Minister from the Dutch church, Dr Dillié, Chandler Captain De Jong, Harbourmaster van Leewen, Master Telegrapher Schruit, Lloyd's Agent Schuit . . . almost everyone who was important in Anjer was in Joost's house.

Kerta knew that besides the general store, Li Yang had several other buildings and Ma said that he was almost as rich as Lloyd's Agent Schuit. He was the unofficial mayor of the Chinese Quarter. Assistant Resident Thomas Buijs was supposed to be a Rajah, ruling over everyone on the coast of Sunda Strait, but nearly everyone ignored him. But nobody ignored the Imam. He was only the leader in Anjer's small mosque but he was *absolutely* certain about everything, and everyone – even the Dutch – knew that he was very powerful. And now he was imperiously crooking his finger at Pa.

'Oh, um.' Pa walked slowly towards him.

The Imam tugged his beard. 'I haven't seen you in the mosque for a while . . .'

'We've had a little trouble with the volcano.'

'Allah is not concerned with little imps on little islands. He is concerned with you.'

'I am sorry. I pray at the top of Fourth Point.'

Li Yang smiled. 'It is a mighty minaret.'

The Imam looked at him with a frown, as if he was working out whether he was being mocked.

But then Assistant Resident Thomas Buijs snorted. 'It is not a minaret, it is a Dutch lighthouse.'

'There is a cross there too,' Jacob said gently as he drifted past.

The Imam frowned lightly and then he shrugged. 'Of course a lighthouse can be a minaret just as a *proa* can be a mosque.' But then he turned to Pa. 'But come to my house soon.'

Then Pa was caught by Lloyd's Agent Schuit and pulled into another group and Kerta followed.

'They say the captain has bad news for us,' Schuit said, wiping his face with his sleeve. 'Is Krakatoa looking worse from the lighthouse?'

Jacob turned to Pa. 'I told them that we can't see anything now, it's a fog of ash, but I think it is settling down. Would you say?'

Pa smiled. 'It is easier to clean the panes.'

'That what I thought too,' Master Telegrapher Schruit said.

Harbourmaster van Leewen waved his stinking pipe around. 'I don't know what this captain has to say. I had a word with an English lad who sailed a *proa* near Krakatoa a month ago and he didn't see anything special. I have studied the plumes of smoke from Krakatoa and there's nothing in there. The captain could go to any active volcanoes in the bubbling Dutch Indies and see a better display . . .'

Suddenly Kerta was looking at Tuan Joost's deeply troubled face across the room. Tuan Joost was stabbing his finger at him. His mouth said something soundless as he hurried towards him. Kerta stepped back in alarm when he saw Jan behind Joost.

'I wanted to see you,' Joost said quickly.

'Yes . . .'

'About two weeks ago you brought a telegram here.'

'Yes.' Kerta saw Jan's eyes widening.

'Did you know what it said?'

'Said . . . ?' Kerta saw Jan shaking his head furiously at him. 'I didn't see the message, Tuan. They gave me the envelope and I gave it to you.'

'You're sure?'

Kerta nodded.

Tuan Joost grunted and walked away.

Jan came over. 'I didn't tell him that I told you what the message said. About the gunpowder.'

'Oh.'

'Did you tell anyone? About the gunpowder.'

'No. Why?'

'Someone has stolen it.'

Kerta took a quick breath. 'From the depot? I thought that was impossible.'

'Someone dug under the wall and waited.'

Kerta remembered the muddy Hasan. 'Ah.'

'You sure you didn't tell anyone?'

'Did you tell the police where Hasan's pa was hiding?'

'What?'

'The time Hasan's pa was blaming you Dutch for

Krakatoa, and the police came with *Berouw*. And that gun-boat shot him. Did you tell the police?'

'Do you think that?'

Kerta hesitated and then nodded.

Well, I didn't.'

'All right.'

'I only told Papa . . .'

Kerta and Jan stared at each other for a long time.

'Hell, hell, hell . . .' Jan walked away. Kerta did not stop him.

Then Tuan Joost pushed the door to the house wide open. 'The captain is here . . .'

A tall sunburned man in the uniform of the Dutch army stepped into the house, to be clapped and presented with a drink.

'There you are.' Tuan Joost waved his hand at the officer. 'You want to know what the volcano is doing right now? See Captain Ferzenaar, the man who went to Krakatoa only two days ago – brave enough to go there by himself.'

Assistant Resident Buijs hunched his back.

The captain looked at him and shrugged. 'No, you mean stupid.'

'How bad is the volcano?' Tuan Joost asked.

The captain sucked his teeth. 'I really don't know. It depends what it was like in the past. I did put my foot on the higher hill of Krakatoa – Rakata – but I didn't stay there. There were still trees and bushes on the top, but it was a frightening place.'

'My son has been there, at Rakata.' Mrs Joost pushed Jan before him. 'When it all started.'

Jan nodded furiously, looking away from Kerta. 'That was scary, with explosions all over the place –'

'When did you go?'

'Ah . . .' Jan looked at Kerta. 'May. Halfway through May.'

'May? It's a long time ago, isn't it?'

'My son has been there later.' Pa pointed.

The captain cocked an eyebrow as he heard Kerta's story and then shook his head. 'The crater? All of you went up to the crater? That's madness. It's quiet, but I wouldn't go there now. But you saw only one crater firing?'

'Yes. Big smoke.'

'At Perboewatan. Alone.'

'Yes.'

The Harbourmaster said, 'And there was a seaman who sailed near Krakatoa a couple of weeks ago and he wasn't impressed.'

'Yes?'

'A lad called Dalby, Liverpool English; with such a thick accent you'd think he was an Eskimo. His ship, the barque *Hope*, was picking up cargo in Anjer for a few days so he asked me where he could get a *proa* to cross the Sunda Strait. I pointed him to the canal.'

'What did he see?' said the captain.

'He said that Krakatoa was very quiet, just chimney smoke – but he said there were two. There was Perboewatan and –'

'Rakata. The high peak is smoking. They are both gentle, and I wouldn't worry about them, but there's more. After I had a good look at the middle volcano, Danan, I wanted to go home. Oh, I finished the map of the island, but I anchored on the other side of Verlaten. Next day I came back.'

'What did you see?' Tuan Joost said.

'Danan is erupting too, and there's more. I only saw the southern slopes of Danan, but I saw pink smoke from vents all over the rock. I could count fourteen vents. The island is beginning to collapse . . .'

* * *

After the party Jacob, Ma and Pa walked towards the lighthouse. They kept on talking about the danger from Krakatoa. But Kerta trailed after them, thinking of gunpowder and Hasan.

the bang

THE BANG was his trigger.

Kerta thought of Hasan a great amount. He tried to put himself into Hasan's sandals again, tried to imagine Pa being shot by that gunboat, tried to imagine wanting revenge. But it didn't work. Pa was a lighthouse keeper, that gunboat captain wouldn't dare and he – dumb Kerta – couldn't light a firework! All he knew was he was like Hasan, not like Jan, because he and Hasan were not Dutch.

He thought about Hasan and Jan as he delivered messages around Anjer and also took messages back to the telegraph office, but it wasn't helping.

Almost every time a ship came from Krakatoa, Kerta was working, but his mind was elsewhere. As the ships sailed close to Anjer they sent messages by semaphore or with flags on the rigging and Lloyd's Agent Schuit wrote them all down for Kerta to carry to Master Telegrapher Schruit. When the *Madura*, the *Bay of Naples,* the *Princess Wilhelmina* and even the *Loudon* streamed past, their flags had a bright carnival air, but their messages were the all the same. The ships were covered in ash as they moved near the island and the sea was thick with pumice.

But Kerta was trying to work out what to do about Hasan . . .

All right, he had the gunpowder. He was not going to blow up the Joost house. He didn't know if Tuan Joost had told the police and he wouldn't use it on Jan – he had all the time to get him with his knife. The thing is, he didn't know who brought the soldiers and *Berouw* to get his pa. But he knew who shot his pa.

He wanted to sink *Berouw*.

And what do you do to stop him? Tell Joost and get Hasan chained with his pa? Tell my pa? And what would he do? You just don't know. Hasan is Acehnese, almost as the same as Javanese. And what do you care if he sinks the paddleboat anyway? You'd cheer.

But, can he? He would fire one cannonball and it would miss and those four heavy guns would turn to the fort. The guns would obliterate the fort as Hasan scurried away.

There was nothing to do . . .

But on Thursday Kerta saw a couple of messages that complicated things. One told him *Berouw* would be away in Sumatran waters, which was good. Another told him that *Loudon* would be dropping anchor at Anjer on Sunday to pick up coolies. And that could be trouble. If Hasan couldn't shoot his cannonball on *Berouw* he might fire at the anchoring *Loudon*. And Captain Lindemann.

Kerta was worrying about that as he walked towards the mosque when he heard the bang.

The bang was not particularly loud, but people around Kerta turned to Krakatoa. But *he* looked towards the fort, and saw a puff of smoke and a splash in the water fifty metres from the fort. He ran through the confused people, past the grey British monument, and the mosque, to the fort. There was nobody there.

He stopped and saw a faint curl of mist come from a cannon, the cannon he had seen Hasan sitting on a long time ago. Several Dutchmen hurried into the fort and Harbourmaster van Leewen squinted at him. Kerta realised that he was trying to work out how Kerta had caused that explosion.

But Dr Dillié smiled at him. 'Ah, Kerta, did you see anything?'

He hesitated.

'No? Nothing at all? Ah, well.' The doctor strolled towards the cannons.

The Harbourmaster shrugged. 'It was Krakatoa. It was just an echo, nothing to worry about.' He turned away and walked from the fort.

The doctor stopped for a moment, frowning at the mist wafting from the barrel of a cannon but then he followed the Harbourmaster.

Kerta stayed and looked around. He was feeling the heat of the cannon when Hasan popped out from the long grass around the mud parapet.

'Did you see it? Straight as an arrow! Wham!' Hasan skidded his hands against each other.

'What were you trying to hit?'

Hasan glanced at Kerta's Dutch peaked cap. 'You're going to tell them.'

'I didn't tell them when you thieved the gunpowder.'

'How do you know?'

'I figured.'

Hasan looked at him then slowly nodded. 'All right, then. I had trouble getting the gunpowder before. I thought I'd get it at Li Yang's with the fireworks, but there was nothing.'

'Wrong time.'

'I didn't take anything else, anyway. But Pa helped – yeah, he can do things even with the chains and the guards – I sneaked to a bush when he was resting on the road work and asked him where could I find gunpowder. He wanted to know what I was trying to do, but a guard was coming up so he only got to say, "Dig under the depot and wait." But that was enough, hey?'

'I suppose.'

'I had the gunpowder but I didn't know how to fire – until now. I tried to get it going for more than a week, but finally I worked it out. I found this little hole on the barrel of the cannon for a light to reach the gunpowder . . . Now that Dutch gunboat can be sunk by a Dutch cannon! Where is it?'

'*Berouw* . . .' Kerta pointed across the water.

'You're not trying to stop me?'

Kerta looked down at the Dutch cap in his hand and then lifted his head. 'You are only after *Berouw*, right?'

'Yes.'

'No other ship, no other person?'

'*Berouw* is good enough.'

'I don't care about *Berouw*. You can have it. But it is now in Lampong Bay.'

'Oh.'

'Anchored near Telok Betong, maybe waiting for *Loudon*. She comes here for a lot of coolies to build a lighthouse in Telok Betong. She is also carrying three hundred convicts from Batavia.'

'Ah . . .' Hasan walked to the cannon. 'We can wait.'

Kerta smiled at Hasan and left. He knew that there would be trouble coming, but not yet. He had time to work things out. He could live with that.

∗   ∗   ∗

'Kerta!'

The shout sounded like Master Telegrapher Schruit, but it wasn't coming from the office. Kerta looked around.

'Here!'

Then Kerta spotted him, waving from the hotel veranda. He seemed to have been looking through Lloyd's Agent Schuit's brass telescope, and now he was sweeping his arm to bring Kerta to the hotel. All the weeks Kerta had carried Master Telegrapher Schruit's messages he had never heard a hint of concern in his voice, but this time it was different. He ran to the hotel as his mind raced, trying to work out what had happened.

Had he made a terrible mistake with the telegrams, like losing one, or worse – giving one to the wrong person?

He skidded through the doorway of the hotel, galloped up the stairs, and ran onto the veranda. Master Telegrapher Schruit was thumping his fist lightly on the telescope as he glared at the dark smoke.

'It's Krakatoa,' he said.

'Oh,' said Kerta dully. 'It wasn't Krakatoa, Tuan. There was echo . . .'

'What are you talking about?'

'The bang.'

'The bang? That was nothing. A ship cleaning a cannon, someone had a birthday, I don't care. This morning did anyone at the lighthouse see anything from the volcano?'

'No . . .'

Master Telegrapher Schruit shook his head and poked the telescope. 'You look through this damned thing, your eyes are better than mine.'

Kerta stepped across and peered, seeing a blurred ring around the Fourth Point and smoke beyond. 'Um, what am I looking for, Tuan?'

'Can you see Rakata – the high peak?'

Kerta squinted as he fiddled with the focus, but finally shook his head.

'No sign? Maybe Willem's right.'

Kerta stepped back from the telescope and waited.

Master Telegrapher Schruit looked at him. 'Willem Beyerinck from Kalimbang sent us a message. He told us about the fishermen's escape when Perboewatan first erupted and he checked their story about a steaming beach by *going* there. Willem gets things right, which is bad.'

He turned to the boiling black smoke. 'Willem says that Rakata has lost its top.'

perfect sunday

But nothing else happened on Friday, or on Saturday, and Sunday morning was perfect. The sun slid from the still jungle into a clear blue sky, the *proas* were catching a light breeze to scud over rippling waves, ships wandered across Sunda Strait, the gulls wafted around Fourth Point. Krakatoa was still hidden by its ash fog and a black column was still towering in the sky above, but the smoke and the ash were not anywhere near Anjer. Ma, Rara and one of the Brothers, Wayan, quickly put up the washing to make use of the clear air before breakfast.

Even Hasan was not angry. After breakfast Carver helped the Brothers at the lighthouse as Jacob wandered off with his walking stick on his shoulder and the twins running around his legs. Kerta's family joined them, drifting through the kampong towards Anjer. Kerta was lagging behind, clinking his coins in his pocket and talking with the twins, when he saw Hasan moving through the coconut trees towards him. He looked worried.

'Is this bad?' Adam said quickly.

177

'No, not anymore. I don't think.' But Kerta pushed Dewi on. She was talking with her doll, Upya.

'Kerta . . . ?' Hasan was uncertain.

Kerta stopped on the road and waited as the twins pulled Dewi away.

'I can't find Pa,' Hasan said. 'He was working near Merak. I could get there. But now there's nothing.'

'Oh . . .'

'Do you know something?'

For a moment Kerta hesitated. He was supposed to keep the secrets in the messages, but he had told Hasan things before and Hasan wasn't looking at him like he was a Dutch dog anymore. Kerta wanted to keep it that way. 'Maybe there's something.'

'What, then?'

'Remember the *Loudon* will bring about three hundred convicts from Batavia to Sumatra today?'

Hasan shook his head. 'Pa wasn't in Batavia.'

'But the *Loudon* is coming to Anjer this afternoon to pick up some coolies and a few convicts.'

'A few convicts . . .'

'That's all I know.'

A blaze of light swept over Hasan's face. 'He's there!'

He jogged away. Then he looked back. '*Loudon* goes to Telok Betong, hey! *Berouw* is there.'

*   *   *

Kerta joined the others crossing the bridge. They met Assistant Resident Thomas Buijs with his large Alsatian in the avenue of figs – *warignen* trees; they talked with Lloyd's Agent Schuit, who was wearing a smart cream tropical suit and a Panama hat instead of his worn shirt and denim trousers. Madam Schuit had come out of the bar of the hotel in a bright white blouse and long black skirt and she whirled a gold parasol while she talked with Ma and Jacob's wife. There were many parasols on the Waterfront, and a few Chinese women wearing cheongsams.

They waved at Master Telegrapher Schruit, who was admiring the house he had purchased and taking notes. They talked with Dr Dillié, who was sniffing flowers, and his battered bag was nowhere to be seen. They joined the Joost family and Pilot de Vries outside the pilot station. Tuan Joost was still wearing his white cap, but with a brown tropical suit. It fact, everyone in the town seemed to be dressed up for this sunny Sunday morning – except for Pilot de Vries, because he was working. He had a far bigger telescope than Lloyd's Agent Schuit's, and he read the flags from ships coming towards Anjer. If a ship captain needed a pilot to moor in Anjer's roadstead at Merak Bay or help sail past Thwart-the-Way, Pilot de Vries putted his old boat towards the ship. He had been working on the water barge for today's coolies.

They nattered about ships, Master Telegrapher Schruit's house, the slowing down of the volcano and the coolies going to Telok Betong, and then the church bell rang. The families of Joost, Schuit and Jacob walked past the hotel, picked up Schruit, walked past Joost's house, past the Dutch cemetery and into the wooden church. And Pa led Ma, Dewi and Kerta down the coconut-shaded Waterfront to the mosque. On the way Pa remarked that the morning breeze had died.

Ma glared at the smear over Krakatoa. '*That* better not get over my washing . . .'

The Imam saw the family stepping into his white mosque and muttered, 'Allah be praised.'

*　　*　　*

Pa suggested that they drop into Baha's coffee shop. They planted themselves round an outside table, got sarsaparillas for Kerta and Dewi and black coffee for Pa and Ma. They were joined by Jacob and his twins.

Baha showed them his full Indian headdress, eagle-feathers marching down his back. 'My son sent me this, and Li Yang is very jealous. After all, his Indian is only a piece of wood.'

Dirck touched the feathers with awe. 'Your son must be a great Indian fighter – as good as General Custer! Did he grab this from a chief's head in a battle? I bet.'

Baha glanced at Kerta and winked. 'Oh, probably.'

Suddenly Kerta remembered that Jacob had said Baha with his little coffee shop would know more secrets than an army of spies. 'Um, Tuan Baha, do you know what a velocipede is?'

Baha tilted his head and frowned.

No, he doesn't know, Kerta thought. 'Mac is going to bring me that, but nobody knows what it is . . .' He shrugged.

'Ah,' Baha nodded. 'Yes, the velocipede, it is a two-wheeled riding machine. It is supposed to be faster than walking, but everything is made of wood. It is also called the boneshaker.' Baha smiled as he moved away from the table and watched the world drift past.

While the old people chattered, Dewi discussed the colour of her dress with Upya, the twins argued about cowboys and Indians and Kerta looked around. He saw Master Telegrapher Schruit, Lloyd's Agent and Madam Schuit having lunch on the hotel veranda, Pilot de Vries reading a newspaper in his station, Hasan slouching near the pilot's station, and several coolies walking from the Chinese Quarter to the Water Wharf. He looked out across Sunda Strait to a few late *proas* drifting towards their kampongs, and watched a barque slide towards Thwart-the-Way. Further out was the *Gouverneur-Generaal Loudon*; its yellow funnel was streaming smoke behind it.

Jacob grunted and pointed at both ships. 'The breeze has moved –'

Suddenly a deep thundering rumble passed over the streets of Anjer.

darkness

For a long moment everyone was quiet and then the rumble died.

Jacob looked at Pa. 'Earthquake?'

But Pa was turning to the haze of Krakatoa and Kerta saw Pilot de Vries throwing his newspaper aside to swing his heavy telescope there. The coolies had stopped on the road.

'All right, it's playing up again.' Jacob shrugged at his boys as he took out his pocket-watch. 'Just over one o'clock – we might think about going home.'

Adam looked at Pa. 'It's all right, isn't it?'

'Ah.' Pa shifted his eyes. 'Oh, yes.'

Master Telegrapher Schruit hurried from the hotel veranda to Pilot de Vries's station, talked to him briefly, and went into his telegraph office.

Then Kerta saw a thick shoot of white steam spurt from the fog of Krakatoa. As the steam barrelled into the sky there were loud crashes and more violent rumbling.

'Upya doesn't like the angry sound,' Dewi said.

'Let's go, Papa.' Adam tugged Jacob's shirt.

'Ah, what's wrong with you?' Dirck said. 'It's only bangs.'

Li Yang was staring at the steam with his hand on the head of the wooden Indian. 'It's not as bad as May, is it?' he said, as if he was talking to the Indian. Tuan Baha was slowly twisting a dishcloth near him and nobody answered. Jacob stamped his walking stick, stood up and both families moved away from Baha's coffee house. As Kerta walked along the Waterfront he watched the eruption directly in front of him with a terrible fascination.

Steam was now belching from the volcano in huge balloons that chased each other into the deep sky. The thunder was more frequent and louder with each step he took nearer.

Kerta tried to compare this with the other time, but then he was *there*, on Krakatoa. This time he was far away, but he could hear the power in those explosions. He looked sideways to Pa and knew that Pa felt this was worse. Pa started to say something to Kerta, but Ma caught his eye and he shut up. Kerta realised that Pa stopped for Dewi and the twins. He was learning.

They paused near the telegraph office to let two soldiers and three clanging convicts go past. Kerta recognised Hasan's father as one of the convicts. Then he saw Hasan dart across in front of them to the coal bunkers. One of the soldiers slowed and pulled his gun from his shoulder.

Kerta suddenly forgot about Krakatoa. Something terrible was going to happen right this minute, and he had caused it . . .

But nothing happened. Hasan's pa lifted his hand carefully to touch his mouth with his finger. He seemed not to see Hasan. The soldier with the unslung gun watched Hasan as he came closer to the bunker, but then he shoved his rifle back onto his shoulder. Hasan was only a boy.

Kerta could see Hasan's mouth twitching as his father reached him, but he seemed to be uncertain what to do. His pa kept his eyes locked on the approaching *Loudon* until he was very close to the coal bunker. Then he turned quickly and winked at his son before clinking towards the water barge. Hasan blinked at his retreating back, then slowly smiled.

But as the convicts and coolies drifted onto the Water Wharf a dark shadow swept across Sunda Strait. Kerta saw that Krakatoa's white boiling steam had changed into black smoke and it was spreading across the sky.

'There's Carver and Rara,' said Pa in slight surprise.

'Really? Where?' Jacob saw the pair near the hotel and hurried to them. 'What are you doing here?'

'It's all right.' Carver was talking quickly. 'The Brothers are looking after the lighthouse – we took a short break. We won't stay.'

'Just go now.'

'Yes, straight away . . .'

They moved away.

The shadow came over the streets of Anjer, suddenly chilling the afternoon. The sun was now a glimmer in the black cloud and the once deep-blue water was now becoming lead.

Pa nodded at the water as if it was telling him something.

'I don't like this,' Jacob said.

Pa said quietly, 'The Antoe Laoet is coming.'

Jacob looked at him with annoyance but said nothing.

Kerta saw Jacob's face changing from grim to sullen to a death's head with eyes glittering through a shadow. He was alarmed and then he realised that everyone's faces had became dark. The streets of Anjer had dimmed and the sun had become nothing more than a grey wash in the black smoke. The coolies clutched at each other on the Water Wharf and began a hollow wail.

'It's changing,' Ma said softly. 'The water.'

'It'll be all right, Ma?' Dewi grabbed her hand.

Ma didn't say anything, but she scooped Dewi up and hurried towards the telegraph office.

The dark strait was now surging up and down, as if there was something down below the surface. Angry swells began to rush onto the Water Wharf, making Pilot de Vries's loaded barge buck, and the coolies shrieked. The swells thudded onto the beach and crashed against the Waterfront's coconut trees. Two coolies in the barge tried to climb back onto the wharf, but Pilot de Vries cast off and churned towards the *Loudon* in Merak Bay.

A heavy man lurched into Kerta and savagely pushed him sideways. Pa moved towards the man in anger, but Jacob stopped the charging man with a solid hand on his shoulder.

'Easy, easy, it's not so bad,' Jacob said calmly.

The man jerked his head up and Kerta saw that he was Tuan Joost. 'Get out of the way!'

Jacob stepped back and tried to smile. 'A bit of smoke. You were back there; you should be used to it now.'

'No, no . . .' Joost stumbled past and then looked back.

Kerta looked into his eyes and felt an icy shiver. He had seen those staring eyes before, when Krakatoa woke and the water-spouts slid towards *Goliath*. Then Joost had fixed his eyes at them and spun *Goliath* away, but now those eyes were carrying something more than fear . . .

'Look at it!' Joost waved his arms at the wailing coolies, at the spreading blackness, the thundering volcano, the shivering sea. 'You haven't seen this before!'

The water was retreating from the beach, like a king tide but incredibly fast. Kerta saw the seas sucking away from the deep rocks, leaving frantic fish flapping in the mud. The coolies were left standing on the skeleton of the wharf while the barge, jammed with Chinese men, women, soldiers, and the shackled convicts, was racing away from them. The people on the Water Wharf and the barge were reaching hopelessly towards each other.

The light was failing. There was only a slither of blue sky far beyond Thwart-the-Way and the thick black smoke was rolling over that. As *Loudon* dropped an anchor in Merak Bay she turned on her navigation lights. Within half an hour the bright early afternoon had become night.

Dutch people around the Waterfront were putting out their hands and looking up.

'Pharaoh . . .' mumbled Joost.

The blackness of the sky seemed to be peeling, drifting down shadows over Anjer.

'Pharaoh saw this on the night his first son died.' Joost looked down to his hands and saw that they were covered with black ash. He shook his head. 'It's worse than that. It's the end of the world!' He lurched away.

end of the world

 THE Assistant Resident, Thomas Buijs, brushed past Jacob as he moved towards the telegraph office, muttering, 'The end of the world. He could be right . . .' He looked deeply frightened.

Ma jerked Pa's arm. 'We have to go.' Her face had blanched under her brown skin, and Dewi was clutching to her neck as if she was a blind monkey baby.

But then Harbourmaster van Leewen pushed through some coolies and waved his pipe at Joost's shrinking back. 'It is *not* the Day of Judgement!' he shouted and people gathered. 'It is just a normal volcanic eruption. It happens all the time in the Dutch Indies. It's a bit dark, but it will blow over, take it from me. Just ignore it, as we have in the past.'

Suddenly Kerta liked the blowhard Harbourmaster. He could say anything about lazy, stupid Javanese boys if he was right now.

And then Kerta saw that Jacob was looking beyond him to the Pilot as he nudged his barge against the *Loudon* and coolies began to climb the sea steps. As if nothing had changed. And even Jacob smiled a little as he began to lead the way to the lighthouse.

Kerta shuffled quickly after Jacob, thinking that he would get away from this black afternoon. All he had to do was walk through the Dutch Quarter, cross the stone bridge, cut through the kampong and he was home. In the closed hut he could forget the darkness, the falling ash and the berserk water because he wouldn't see them. The booming and the crashes? They were something that was distant like a thunderstorm, nothing to do with him. He was almost a step from home . . .

Master Telegrapher Schruit leaned from the door of his office. 'Ndora, I need Kerta . . .'

Kerta hunched his back.

Pa glanced at the swelling water and shook his head.

Master Telegrapher Schruit looked tired. 'I told Batavia about Krakatoa and they want us to keep the office open until seven.'

Pa shifted his eyes to Ma and she jerked her head. She was carrying Dewi and rocking slowly. Dewi was pushing her face against Ma's cheek, crushing Upya in her hand and she was crying in silence. 'No, I'm sorry.'

'I understand.'

Kerta closed his eyes for a moment and then he stepped up to Pa. 'I have to. I am a Telegram Boy.' Almost as important as a lighthouse keeper.

Pa looked at his son and hesitated.

'I want to go, now,' Ma said quickly.

Pa screwed up his lips and then sighed. 'All right, you can stay, but watch it very carefully. When you come home it may be a good idea to use the rope bridge . . .'

Kerta walked to the office and then turned to watch his family moving through the seething crowd, wishing that he was leaving with them. The Master Telegrapher patted him on the shoulder and pulled the door open. Telegrapher Berg was clicking on the brass key under a hissing kerosene lamp.

Berg pushed himself away from the key. 'I told Batavia that down here it is so dark you can't see your hand before your eyes.'

'Well, that's not quite true . . .' The Master Telegrapher turned to the wall as if he was looking through it.

Kerta felt something big was moving.

Master Telegrapher Schruit turned quickly. 'The sea. What was it doing before, coming in?'

'The tide was going out.'

'It can't be!' The Master Telegrapher lurched outside.

Kerta followed him and heard the sound of rushing water in the dark. He could see the *Loudon*'s glimmering lights and its silhouette, but he couldn't see how the sea looked. People were shouting.

The Master Telegrapher peered into the dark. 'I think – Jesus!'

A brown wave crashed against the coal bunker and barrelled towards them. Kerta could hear shrieks and desperate scrabbling near him as he ran. The water clutched at his ankle, but then fell away. He took long one step, realised that he was clear and thought about the Master Telegrapher. He turned as the panting runner crashed into his back.

'Sorry, sorry.' The Master Telegrapher held Kerta, rocked a bit and let go. His trousers were clinging to his skinny calves.

They stood together as the wave receded, dragging a woman along the beach until two men caught her and pulled her to her feet. Krakatoa boomed across the strait in anger.

The Master Telegrapher opened his hand and watched the falling ash and small pumice spread in his palm. 'It is going to be a bad day.'

But Pilot de Vries rode his barge on a sudden swell to the Water Wharf, and tossed lines to the coolies. The barge thudded violently against the wharf's poles and the coolies moved away until one of them, a young man, threw his tied basket into the barge and leaped after it. The others waited until the barge dipped, but then they scrabbled across. One woman almost fell between the grinding of the barge's side and the wharf, but two men grabbed her arm and pulled her on board.

Kerta watched the men and women coolies as they walked past the telegraph office, and they all looked very frightened. But they still kept moving towards the tossing barge. Some of them were carrying small baskets of their possessions tied to the end of long poles on their right shoulders and Kerta wondered how they could climb the sea steps of the *Loudon* with them. Then he was tapped on the shoulder and turned to see a haggard Jan.

'What are you doing? Working *now*?' Jan's eyes were wide.

'Because of today.' Kerta nodded in the direction of Krakatoa. 'Batavia wants us to keep on going.'

'Papa thought that Schruit would be doing that. That's why I'm here.'

'A telegram?'

Jan looked at him. 'Papa thinks that maybe the world mightn't end today, but the Batavia merchants shouldn't send stuff to him at the moment. God, it's terrible, isn't it?'

Master Telegrapher Schruit looked back at Jan. 'It is. But maybe it's not all bad . . . Your father wants to send a telegram?'

'Several.'

Master Telegrapher Schruit nodded and turned back to watch the loading of the barge.

'Oh, hell.' Jan had glanced at the water tank. 'Is he still after me?'

Kerta followed Jan's eyes and saw Hasan had moved from the coal bunker to the shadow of the water tank. And then he knew what Hasan was trying to do. 'No, don't worry about him now,' he said quietly to Jan.

As a group of coolies moved towards the tank he began to raise his hand in a farewell to Hasan. But Hasan was pulling a heavy sack from the back of the tank and hefted it onto his back.

Kerta stared at the sack and his hand dropped.

'What's he carrying?' Jan said.

'I don't know,' Kerta lied.

For a moment Hasan and Kerta looked at each other without a wave or a nod. Kerta standing next to his Dutch master and his Dutch friend and Hasan with his bag and his father in chains in the bobbing *Loudon*. They were not enemies, not now, but they were not friends. The gulf was too great.

Hasan slid in with the coolies. A wispy man cocked his head at him and then put his hand on his shoulder and they walked together towards the barge, as Hasan lugged his bag of gunpowder.

'All right, we'd better get those telegrams going.' The Master Telegrapher turned away from the strait and opened the office door for Jan.

Kerta followed the Master Telegrapher into his office as Krakatoa cracked twice. He was hunching while he closed the door, but soon he began to feel a little safer. The white walls of the office were keeping back the dark water and Orang Aljeh's roars. The clicking of the telegraph, the ticking of the wall clock, and the quiet hissing of the kerosene lamp told him that nothing had changed.

Jan placed the notes before the gaunt Telegrapher Berg, who scribbled with his thick pencil and worked with the brass knob.

'It is good when we can send people's messages while we wait,' the Master Telegrapher said, and took the money from Jan.

'Well . . .' Jan looked at Kerta awkwardly. 'I guess I have to go.'

Reluctantly Kerta went outside with Jan and heard the wailing again.

Jan was watching his face. 'Papa was like that, wasn't he?'

Kerta shrugged.

'Do you think your ghost is coming for us?'

Kerta looked sharply at Jan. He thought that Jan was sneering at him but his eyes were wide. 'I –' Then he remembered how Pa had been with frightened Adam. 'It'll be all right, Jan. Pa said so.'

'It's just – you heard Papa and the others.'

'The Harbourmaster said Krakatoa will cool down, like the last time.'

Jan tried to make a weak smile. 'Papa maybe too.' He shrugged and walked away towards his house.

Kerta turned to *Loudon* and saw the shadows of coolies slithering up the sea steps and he thought he saw Hasan with them. Pilot de Vries pulled his barge away. The ship's anchor was hauled up. *Loudon* hooted defiantly at the rumbling volcano, the yellow funnel coughed black smoke into the sullen sky and bucketed towards Kampong Bay.

Kerta was surprised when he stepped into the telegraph office and saw that the wall clock showed only 2.45 p.m.

* * *

The quiet office stayed open for the afternoon. Telegrapher Berg and Master Telegrapher Schruit sent messages to Batavia as Krakatoa fired. When there was a thundering on the tiled roof Kerta put his head out of the office and saw that the street was being hit by large fragments of pumice. He told that to the others, and Batavia learned that Anjer was being bombarded by 'hails of pumice'.

Krakatoa thundered through the hours, but the rain of pumice dropped to coarse ash until Master Telegrapher Schruit decided to send Kerta to get a snack from the Chinese Quarter. Kerta was reluctant to step out of the comfort of the office, but he thought it would be all right if he didn't look at the volcano. He was wrong.

As he pulled the door open he heard distant screaming. He hesitated for a moment, then he stepped into the street. Ash drifted into his face but he could see a few Javanese were waving at the strait. The sea had become worse since *Loudon* left; waves were coming into Anjer's sheltered roadstead, clashing with the rushing ebb tide. A big fishing boat had broken away from its mooring and some fishermen were trying to reach it with small *proas*.

But the wailing and cries further along the Waterfront seemed to be independent from the Javanese. Kerta turned a corner and saw a milling mob of people on the beach and in the water. There were several boats bobbing in the shallows, with Chinese families trying to clamber onto them. A woman threw a small boy into a *proa* and beat her hands onto her thighs. Li Yang ran from his shop with a box under his arm, bustling his wife and their three children towards a large boat. For an instant he looked at Kerta with a blank face, then he was gone.

Kerta saw that there was no shop in the Waterfront open – including Baha's café – so he moved away from the water. The Chinese Quarter was closing as he went to the market, almost deserted, but he found a satay man putting away his grill. He was looking at the dark sky and the falling ash, but then he looked at the coins in Kerta's hand, and fired up the coals again.

While Kerta waited he saw two people moving quickly in the shadows at the edge of the market furthest away from the bay. For a moment one of them looked like Carver and he started to call for him, but of course it couldn't be. Carver and Rara had gone back to the lighthouse . . .

Another crash from Krakatoa shook the air. He groped his way back to the office with the chicken slivers and peanut sauce.

The Master Telegrapher smiled at him. 'I was worrying about you.'

'Everything is closing. Everyone is running away.'

'Never mind, tomorrow it will change. That smells marvellous. Berg, come over . . .'

The gaunt telegrapher took his hand from the knob and looked back. 'Um.'

'Yes?' said the Master Telegrapher.

'It has died.'

cable

THE Master Telegrapher moved to the table. 'Are you sure?'

Berg thumped the knob and the tiny lightning sparks weren't there. 'I was telling Batavia that the volcano was getting worse, as you said, and then there was nothing.'

'Try Merak.'

Berg nodded and swung round.

Kerta knew what was happening. Merak was a small town further up on the strait, so close to Anjer that you could stroll to it in a morning. The cable went to Merak and then to Batavia and if Berg could contact it, then Batavia had to worry about it, not Anjer.

'No,' Berg said flatly. 'Merak is gone too.'

'Never mind. Have a satay, while I do some thinking.' The Master Telegrapher dipped a stick of singed chicken pieces into the peanut sauce.

They ate in silence with the crashing booms and constant shrieks echoing in their ears. Kerta looked at the Master Telegrapher for a long moment and turned away.

There was a time when he thought Master Telegrapher

197

Schruit was a wizard, reaching to the absolute end of the world with a twitch of his fingers. He had thought this wizard had more power than Orang Aljeh and Antoe Laoet together. But now? Those ghosts had flexed some of their strength this afternoon and shown that Schruit was nothing more than a useless bucket with holes.

'What?' Schruit was studying Kerta.

'Oh, nothing. Nothing, at all.'

Schruit finished a satay stick and turned to Berg. 'We have to go and find out where the cable broke.'

They finished the satays, filled the two lanterns and carried them into the street. A woman was sobbing near the hotel, and people were shrieking on the pier. Kerta tasted the sulphur and felt his hands shuddering.

Schruit looked at him as he locked the office. 'I guess you can go home to your lighthouse, Kerta, now. We won't be taking any messages. Do you want to go?'

Kerta glanced at his hands and knew that he wanted very much to be at that solid white granite pillar, but he lifted his eyes to Schruit and shook his head. 'You might need me . . .'

Schruit sighed softly, then passed his lantern to him. 'Then you lead. Follow the cable.'

Kerta walked carefully away from the Waterfront as the telegraphers peered through the falling ash at the cable swinging between the poles. There was still shouting and howling in the thick, stinking air, but with the warm lantern at his arm that didn't matter so much. They moved to the Great Post Road, crossed through the chaotic Chinese Quarter and skirted the market. For a moment they could hear desperate singing from the mosque, and then they reached the old fort.

Kerta lifted the lantern as they passed the mud parapet. The Dutch soldiers had moved on from the fort, but the telegraph cable still went through it.

Schruit covered his glasses and peered through the ash at the top of the post in the fort's quadrangle. 'It's still all right.' But the cable was jerking, as if trying to free itself from the post.

Kerta could hear waves crashing and wood clashing outside the walls as they moved through the fort. He climbed down the slippery stairs to the canal landing and stopped, his lantern winking feebly over the water.

'Oh,' said Berg numbly.

There were two bridges crossing the canal: a drawbridge leading to a kampong near the open sea, and the solid timber bridge along the Great Post Road. Jammed in the hundred metres of canal between the two bridges were thirty *proas* and a schooner.

They would have been fine in the shelter of the canal in normal times. Now hissing waves had broken the rails on the drawbridge and were crashing on the sides of the canal, hurling the *proas* against the solid timber walls and each other. The small boats were splintering apart, their hulls screaming like animals in a fire. The schooner had snapped its cables, and was driving into the Great Post Road Bridge and crushing boats. Every single boat was being destroyed, but nobody was around the canal to save any of them.

'There!' Kerta pointed at the tossing schooner.

The ship's foremast had snagged the telegraph cable where it crossed over with the bridge. The cable had snapped.

'Perhaps we can pull it off,' Berg said.

They walked along the canal from the fort to the bridge, watching the cable slither on the road, rear high and flog in the air.

'We can't do it.' Schruit shook his head.

Kerta wobbled his head in agreement.

'Well . . .' The gaunt telegrapher studied the curling cable. 'I think I can get it.'

'Don't be daft –'

But Berg leaped at the cable as it writhed on the road and clamped his skinny fingers around it. 'I have got it!'

And then a wave hit the schooner and the foremast whipped Berg from the road as if he was a fish on a line. For a moment he soared into the air, thrashing his legs about with his mouth wide, then he let go of the cable. He flapped his arms, crashed onto the bridge's heavy wooden rail and began to slip towards the wild water.

'Berg!' Schruit rushed to him, but Kerta beat him and grabbed Berg's arms.

Kerta stared into his eyes, thinking, I should have done that, not him!

Schruit snatched an arm as the schooner's bowsprit was wrenched over the rail, only two metres from them.

'Oh, god!' Berg kicked in the air hopelessly.

Schruit and Kerta tried to haul him over the rail, but his body would not move. The white bowsprit chomped at the rail, and Kerta felt the timber cracking. It lurched a metre away and was sliding towards Berg.

Then Berg jerked loose, like a cork from a bottle. He slid over the rail and fell onto Schruit and Kerta as the bowsprit splintered right where he had been.

Then Kerta sat up on the road, looked at Berg's twitching face, the coiling cable, the foremast swaying across the dark night and the bowsprit scraping the rail.

It's like the time you jumped onto the black beach at Krakatoa, he thought. Don't think . . .

Schruit looked at him. 'Kerta –'

Kerta bellowed at the night as he leaped to his feet. He ran at the rail, grabbed the schooner's thick cable forestay, vaulted and spun on the bowsprit. He felt the thudding on the rail through his feet as he pressed his back into the forestay, then, glancing up, he saw it almost reached the top of the high foremast. If he had been a monkey he could have scampered up the forestay to reach the snagged telegraph cable, but he wasn't a monkey so he would have to go the hard way.

He allowed himself to fall forward, clutching the ropes around the bowsprit. The hull of the schooner was throwing black waves against the stone base of the bridge and he was hit by heavy spray, as if the water was trying to clutch him. He scuttled along the bowsprit until he was above the solid deck. The schooner pitched sideways and when he could feel the bowsprit beginning to crack under him he quickly dropped down to the deck.

He staggered past a small cabin, reached the foremast and looked up, but when he realised what he would have to do he wished he hadn't jumped onto the ship. He turned to the glimmering lantern on the bridge. Schruit seemed to be shouting something through the crashing waves and the splintering of the wood. He and Berg were swaying incredibly with the bridge and the buildings . . .

A tin mug skidded across the deck, distracting Kerta, and suddenly the ship was not quite so violent. The ship was still being thrown about violently, but *he* was also being thrown about. It was all about riding the schooner, and all he had to do was concentrate on that. Without looking again at Schruit, he slowly climbed on top of a long cabin to reach the foremast ratlines – the rope ladder mounted on the mast.

Once he started to pull himself on the ratlines he almost felt safe. Every rung of the sailors' ladder was connected to the mast and he was clinging with two hands and two feet, as well as pressing with his knees, legs, stomach, chest and even his head. The mast was still jerking in his arms, but everything else followed the foremast – the other masts, the yards, the rigging, even the stern of the schooner. If he closed his eyes, he could stay there.

But he had to keep moving. He looked up, saw the ash night whipping around the mast and didn't look again. He climbed rung by rung with his eyes locked on the rope before his nose until the ratlines stopped.

His hand groped around the mast, and he looked up, frowning. Two metres of bare mast swayed out of his reach across the dark night sky. There was a line from the top of the mast to the mainmast and the telegraph cable was tangled with it. He looked down – at the twenty metres to deck. He stared as his fingers clamped on the ropes and froze.

For a while nothing happened. Then Kerta heard a deep crack from Krakatoa and he closed his eyes.

It's not so high, he thought. The gallery at the lighthouse is three times higher.

But this is a thin mast on a boat in a storm . . .

Stop it. Just don't look.

Kerta breathed slowly, stared at the flaking white paint on the mast as his hand found the forestay and pulled his body up. He could hear the cable hissing above his head, but he ignored it. His arms embraced the narrowing mast as his feet pushed up until they reached the end of the ratlines. His right foot reached the forestay and then he stopped.

All right, he thought. You have to look up; just don't look at the sky.

Kerta gently lifted his head and saw a loop of the cable curling in the air towards him, as if it was a great snake about to strike. He crouched as the loop thumped loudly at the top of the mast and shook ash down on him. It jerked the mast violently and his foot slipped from the forestay. His chest skidded down the mast until he could tighten his arms on the mast and lock his other leg. Then the loop began to run down the mast to the bridge.

He watched it go and thought bleakly, I can't get the cable off. It's impossible. If I get close it will hit me, it will knock me off the ship. It will kill me. I should have realised that from the bridge. Hasan would be laughing at this – killing myself on the top of a maniac ship for a broken *Dutch* telegraph cable. I ought to give up and climb down.

And then he tilted his head and looked at the cable writhing on the jerking mast. His foot clamped back on the forestay.

Maybe . . .

He moved towards the top, keeping his eyes on the loop. The loop gave the cable the power of a huge bullock whip, but that whip was anchored between the bridge and the top of the foremast. It may be a bullock whip, but it was like the bullock was jerking in its harness. But now he was so close to the cable that he could see it scorching the mast.

He ducked as the loop hissed past his head, felt the mast shake and looked up as the loop snapped and curled away. That was his chance. He slid up, grabbed the cable and tried to move it from the mast. His fingers could feel the throbbing strength in it, but he could not shift it. It was like trying to push over the lighthouse.

He wrenched at it, jerked it, and pounded at it with his fist. Nothing at all, and the loop began to come back. Then the schooner lurched sideways, changing everything. Now the cable was loose around the mast. Kerta wobbled, threw the cable away and clutched the mast. The cable came away from the mast, but now the loop was not tethered anymore. The loop straightened out and aimed itself at his head.

He stared at it numbly, a hopeless mouse before a cobra, then he was stumbling, sliding, falling. The last of the loop hit the top of the mast, but he was gone. For a brief moment the cable and Kerta fell together, but then his left hand snagged the forestay. He began to slide down, his other hand and legs clamped on the wire. He skidded down towards the bridge and Schruit.

night

KERTA'S feet hit the heavy rail. He vaulted to the road and rolled a few times.

Schruit came over to him and crouched down. 'Are you all right?'

'I got it, didn't I? It's all down now, isn't it?'

'You shouldn't have . . .' Schruit frowned. 'Your hand is bleeding.'

Kerta held up his right hand and saw a deep red line across his palm and it was beginning to drip blood. He suddenly felt the throbbing pain, then it spread to the other hand and his legs. He sucked in a quick breath.

'Give us a look.' Schruit took both Kerta's hands and examined them.

'Is it bad?' Berg was holding his ribs.

Schruit looked up to Kerta. 'Can you wiggle your fingers?'

He did.

'It's not bad, but still . . .' Schruit pulled a spotless handkerchief from his pocket and pushed it against Kerta's hand. 'Just press that with both hands. Berg?'

Schruit and Berg hauled Kerta to his feet, with a deep grunt from Berg. They steadied him and then Berg awkwardly laid the cable by the edge of the road.

'He has cracked a rib,' Schruit muttered. 'I thought I might have to carry both of you home. Enough – we'll get you fixed in the hotel.'

'We don't fix the cable?' Kerta said weakly.

Schruit looked at him with an odd expression. 'Um, no, that is for the linemen. I'll have them working on it tomorrow.'

Kerta gave a last glance to the cable and turned away, and realised that he was glad that they were stopping. He realised that he was very tired and his eyes wanted to close. Schruit picked up both lanterns and helped Berg along the deserted road and Kerta trailed after them, their lanterns winking in the drifting ash.

They wandered off the road, but Kerta was not sure when it happened. He just all of a sudden realised that Schruit was talking to the Javanese linemen at his house. Later on Schruit left Berg with his wife. Then Schruit and Kerta returned to the Great Post Road and plodded to the turn-off to the wharfs.

Kerta looked vaguely down the road. 'I've got to go home . . .'

Schruit nodded. 'Yes, of course, but we should fix you up first, all right?'

Kerta looked at the bloody handkerchief in his hands, shrugged and walked with Schruit towards the hotel.

Schruit took a few steps, stopped and frowned. 'Listen, son.'

Kerta slowed. 'I can't hear anything.'

'That's it. The volcano isn't booming anymore. It hasn't done anything since you were up the top of the schooner.'

'Oh.'

'Yes, well.'

Kerta and Schruit looked at each other, both avoiding saying what they were thinking in case the words started Krakatoa off again.

They quietly walked towards the hotel, listening for the volcano.

*   *   *

Madam Schuit was appalled when she saw Kerta. '*This* is how you treat your telegraph boys, Schruit?'

'Do we need Dr Dillié?'

'I think he is running around trying to calm people. We'll treat the boy.'

She hustled him with one of the young cooks into a *mandi* to wash him. Every time he tried to complain the cook threw scoops of water at him until he shut up. The cook pushed him out of the *mandi* with a towel and retreated back to the kitchen. And then Madam Schuit advanced with a dark brown bottle.

It was worse than the top of the schooner's mast. He could smell crocodile and snakeskins in the bottle and when she dabbed the orange liquid on his open wounds it felt like the skin was searing. But she said it was good for killing germs and he could remember when Ma put some herbs on a cut and that hurt, so he hissed through his teeth and put up with it. Finally Madam Schuit bandaged his hands and left him slowly to get dressed.

Then he smelled the steaming curried chicken on the plate the young cook was carrying into the dining room. And he could smell rice, fish, meat, pickles . . . 'Um, I have to go,' he said weakly.

'Well, maybe . . .' Schruit looked at Madam Schuit.

She glanced at Schruit then looked at Kerta. 'Of course the boy cannot go to his lighthouse until he has been fed. His mother would be angry with me if I let him go weak from hunger.'

'And this is a special meal,' Lloyd's Agent Schuit said as he entered. 'He should be here.'

Kerta was led to the table by Lloyd's Agent Schuit. Everyone nodded at him, as if they knew him. Maybe they did, from the lighthouse and the telegrams, but he couldn't remember all of them tonight. He was just too tired. He could remember that some kids, some adults and about seven of them were of the Schuit family. And there was Schruit and the Harbourmaster, and others. But although he was missing names, he managed to master his fork with his bandaged hand to avoid missing anything on the table.

There was rice, steaming white rice. And then curries, bullock curry, fish curry, chicken curry, vegetable curry.

Then there were relishes, pickles, sauces for the curries. And nuts, eggs, fruits . . .

'Well, Kerta, how do you like our *rijsttafel*?' said Lloyd's Agent Schuit.

Kerta nodded happily and then he frowned as he mouthed the odd Dutch word. 'But the dishes tonight are Javanese.'

The Harbourmaster laughed. 'Ah yes, but it took the Dutch to put everything together.'

Madam Schuit glanced at the Harbourmaster in annoyance and turned to Kerta. 'Some Dutch people in Batavia worked out this as a banquet and we thought we would try it tonight.'

'And you, my boy, are a perfect guest tonight,' the Harbourmaster said.

'Oh.' Kerta blinked.

'This banquet is the heart of Java and you are Javanese, and you were on Krakatoa when it started.'

Kerta waited.

'And this . . .' He gestured with his thumb at the plates on the table, 'is a celebration of the end of it.'

Kerta and Schruit stared at each other in horror.

'Oh, come on,' Lloyd's Agent Schuit waved him down. 'Give it a rest.'

Kerta hunched and waited. Any minute now, he thought.

'No, no, not at all.' The Harbourmaster grabbed his glass of yellow wine and lifted it in the direction of the volcano.

'Here's to Krakatoa, a good scare and that's it. I was right about it, just a puff.'

Kerta felt a cool breeze stroking his cheek.

'The Chinese can paddle back, the Arabs can get on with counting their money, the Javanese can stop their wailing –'

A thundering crash shook the wooden hotel.

'Jesus!' Schruit gasped as everyone turned to the pitch black Sunda Strait.

From the sea came a rolling rumble as if it was lifting the water and carrying it across the hotel. A sudden purple light shimmered, dancing high in the sky, followed by violent cracks. The hotel roof was hit by a heavy thump and then there was a steady roar on the tiles, making talk impossible. The night became bright as lightning forked across the sky.

The ghostly light caught the Harbourmaster's face and he was laughing.

'That . . .' he shouted and stabbed his finger at the night. 'That is only a normal thunderstorm!'

✳   ✳   ✳

Kerta opened his eyes slowly and for a moment he didn't know where he was. He was covered with a loose sheet and he was looking at a wobbly hairline crack in a ceiling. He was not at home.

He kicked off the sheet and swung his feet to the wooden floor. Rubbing his face, he saw that he had been sleeping on a fat couch, in the dining room, at the hotel. He couldn't remember how he got on the couch, only that the storm seemed to last a while and the banquet was even longer . . .

Ma! His eyes widened in horror. She would be awake, waiting for him. She would be walking around the huts and the lighthouse; she would be going to the Great Post Road to see if he was on it. She would be shaking Pa out of his sleep and he would do something. He would be hurrying through the kampong to Anjer right now.

Kerta saw his sandals by the couch, slipped his feet into them and pulled the straps onto his heel as he staggered to the stairs. He started to run, heard his elephant charge and slowed down – a little. He shuffled quickly through the deserted bar and out the open door. He saw a small group of men standing around a coconut tree as he twisted towards the road.

'Kerta?' Schruit called quietly, but his voice was clear in the stillness.

Kerta reluctantly turned. 'I have to go.'

Schruit broke away from the men and nodded. 'It's all right. Madam Schuit fixed it.'

'Oh, what?'

Schruit smiled. 'You were too worn out to wobble down the steps let alone the walk to the lighthouse, so she sent a boy to your mother to tell her that you're sleeping in the hotel tonight. All right?'

Kerta looked at Schruit and slowly nodded. 'All right.'

'We're out to see how things are. Look at that. It almost hurts, but I've go to admit that the Harbourmaster seems to be right.'

Kerta looked past the men and saw that the sea was now motionless as a black mirror. There was not a single star in the dark night, but he could sense the movement of shadow clouds drifting. The air was so clean now that he could pick out the white telegraph buoy near the point. He could still smell the sulphur, but it was something that he could ignore, like rotting seaweed.

'I think it is finished,' Schruit said.

Kerta looked at the men under the coconut tree, Lloyd's Agent Schuit leaning back to stretch, the Harbourmaster's face relaxing in the glow of his pipe, the doctor, and they were all peering in the direction of Krakatoa. But there was nothing there, not even a pipe glimmer.

He mumbled something to Schruit and slouched back to the hotel and the couch.

explosions

THE blast threw Kerta out of the couch.

For a moment he thought he was dead. He lay on the floor, staring at the knot in the wood with his ears ringing. He didn't know what it was; only that he had heard something that was louder that anything he had ever heard or imagined in his life.

Feet raced across towards him as he pushed himself from the floor. Schruit grabbed his shoulders and said something, but the ringing was stopping him from hearing the words. Schruit patted him, peered at the grandfather clock in the dining room and hurried back to his bedroom.

Kerta turned to the clock. 4.50. Early morning.

He tried to shake the ringing from his ears but failed and fumbled for his sandals. That enormous explosion had to be Krakatoa, but he had no idea what had happened out there. Only that it was very big.

Schruit came out of his bedroom buttoning his shirt, and clattered down the stairs. Kerta followed him to the beach where they squinted at the fog of the volcano.

Schruit turned to Kerta. 'Can you see anything?

214

I can't see anything . . .'

Now Kerta could hear the words through the ringing, which was dropping away. 'No, I don't think so.'

The morning was beginning to lighten, but it wasn't helping much. A thick fog of ash and smoke had reduced the rising sun to a vague glimmer and was hiding the island, as if a grey curtain had been dropped across Sunda Strait. But the water was much the same. It wasn't as still as he had seen it in the night, but it had little more than ripples troubling its surface.

'Anything?' Lloyd's Agent Schuit leaned from the hotel veranda.

Schruit shook his head. 'Oh, I wish I could be there . . .'

'Really?'

Schruit smiled weakly. 'Well, no. But I must tell Batavia.'

'They know. People in Amsterdam would have been woken by that blast.'

'Maybe, but I've got to contact them. I'm going to the fort to see how the linemen are working on that break.'

'No breakfast?'

Schruit shook his head, waggled his fingers at him and walked away.

Kerta hesitated and then followed him.

Schruit slowed. 'You don't have to come, Kerta. You could go home.'

'I just wanted to see the line back. Then I'll go home.'

'All right.' Schruit deviated to the telegraph office,

opened the door, saw a ribbon of paper from the Morse key, ripped it from the key and shoved it into his pocket. 'I'll read it later.'

Kerta frowned. 'But the cable's broken.'

He nodded as he walked out. 'That came from your cable – Telok Betong, Sumatra, to your lighthouse to here. Probably doesn't say much. Just a mutter to Batavia, but I can't send anything until the main cable is fixed.'

They turned away from the office and saw Pilot de Vries strolling along the Waterfront.

'Good morning.' And then the Pilot realised what he had said and winced. 'Or not. I'd like to hear what the Harbourmaster would say about that bang.'

Schruit shrugged. 'He would say, "What bang?"'

The Pilot laughed lightly as he walked away.

Kerta trailed after Schruit towards the fort.

This is stupid, he thought bleakly. There is nothing to do now, just watch the linemen knit the two halves of the telegraph lines and that is it. So why do you have to see it? Because you brought it down –

The second blast froze them, wooden Indians on the empty road.

Then Schruit slowly turned back, and lifted his eyes to the distant fog. '*What* is happening there?'

Kerta wouldn't look back. 'It's the Orang Aljeh.'

Schruit glanced at Kerta but said nothing. Instead he pulled his pocket watch out and pressed it as if he was trying to find some magic power from it.

Kerta saw his fingers whitening on the closed silver disc and wished he had not noticed. 'It was smaller this time.'

Schruit blinked at the watch and opened it. '5.30. An hour from the last explosion. I wish that our friend Mac was here.' He suddenly smiled. 'And he would wish so too.' He shoved the watch in his waistcoat and walked briskly down the road.

Kerta followed him and saw several people looking at them with frightened eyes from their open doors. And he realised why he had to help Schruit – Master Telegrapher Schruit – to get his line going.

When he went back to Fourth Point he would be walking towards Krakatoa – towards the roar of Orang Aljeh. He would pass a lot of scared people in the kampong, like those people in the doorways here. Kerta saw people wailing, throwing mud over themselves, and he realised that he was one of them. He wanted to start wailing right now.

But once upon a time he had believed that Master Telegrapher Schruit was a wizard, able to reach around the world with his tiny lightning sparks, and he had thought that maybe this wizard could do something against the power of Orang Aljeh and Antoe Laoet . . .

They had snapped his cable to the world by throwing a schooner against the telegraph line, but maybe he could fix it. And there was no one else in Anjer trying to fight them except Master Telegrapher Schruit. Maybe it was a little thing, but if Master Telegrapher Schruit could put the cable back then the Telegram Boy could walk past the wailing people, towards Orang Aljeh, and home.

Kerta could see the schooner drifting in the canal from the distance and its foremast seemed to be slightly tilted. There were two men working on the damaged telegraph line by the corner of the bridge.

'Good, good.' Schruit hurried to them.

One of the men stood up and wiped his hands with a rag as he waited for Schruit.

Kerta slowed as he approached the canal and felt heavy. Beyond some broken poles in the mud, the drawbridge did not exist. The schooner was nudging the bridge with its bow, but the bowsprit was drifting in the air on the side of the ship with only its forestay attached. Last night he had slid down that forestay from the top foremast, but now it was drifting loosely, with the top foremast swaying independently of the ship. The hull of the schooner was covered in savage gashes, but many boats in the canal had suffered more. One *proa* was lying across another, three were awash and one was snapped in two like a twig.

Orang Aljeh and Antoe Laoet had flexed a finger and destroyed Anjer's fleet.

'It's not so bad,' said the lineman to Schruit with a shrug. 'Maybe we will finish with it in an hour, maybe less.'

'That's fine. Batavia will be glad,' Schruit said. 'I'll be waiting over there to get the word from you.'

The lineman nodded. 'Those explosions? I never heard anything like that in my life. You don't know . . . ?'

'No. Only that they came from Krakatoa. But maybe it's over.' Schruit smiled, shrugged and walked across the bridge, reading the ribbon paper from his pocket.

Kerta wandered after him, when he heard his name called from the road. He turned and saw Lloyd's Agent Schuit staggering slightly towards the bridge, and he was carrying a basket. Kerta hurried to his side.

'Here, you carry it now.' Lloyd's Agent Schuit pushed the basket into Kerta's hands and strolled to Schruit.

Schruit was sitting at the bridge rail with an eyebrow cocked.

'Madam Schuit did it,' said Schuit. 'She thought you couldn't last without your tea.' He turned to Kerta and whipped the white cloth from the basket. There was a teapot wrapped in a dishcloth, tin mugs, sugar, a bottle of goat's milk, and a ginger cake.

'Ah, that's lovely.' Schruit patted the rail.

Schuit jumped up to join him and nodded at his *Goliath* near him. 'I have to see what Krakatoa has done.' He took the basket from Kerta.

'It looks all right, I think.'

'It hasn't sunk on me. Sugar?'

'Please, one. But the other side of the Sunda Strait has had a bad time.' Schruit looked up from the ribbon of paper. 'The Controller of Kalimbang, Willem Beyerinck, saw the *Loudon* at 7 pm last night and said he was having trouble with wild rollers.'

Kerta looked up sharply.

'Those rollers were wrecking the *proas* and some houses so he got people and his family up the mountain. And then the Harbourmaster at Telok Betong said *Loudon* had arrived there at 7.30 pm, but Captain Lindemann could not land his convicts and coolies there. The jetty was washed away. The captain gave up and sailed into the rollers to the open Lampong Bay. The gunboat *Berouw* is having trouble – maybe worse.'

'Because of those bloody paddlewheels, right?' said Lloyd's Agent Schuit. 'That gunboat is only good on rivers or still water like a pond.'

'Anyway *Berouw* can't go anywhere until the water calms down. The gunboat is in the shadow of Telok Betong and they have thrown out anchors all over the place. Now they can do nothing but hope.'

'But *Loudon* is all right,' Kerta said.

Schruit ran his finger over the paper. 'The Harbourmaster says that he thought in that storm he saw the ship blazing blue.'

'Oh no . . .'

Lloyd's Agent Schuit patted Kerta on the shoulder with a smile. 'Worried about the captain? Don't. That was in the storm last night. *Loudon* was hit by a blue ball of electricity; it doesn't hurt at all. Sometimes the blue flame stays with a ship for two hours and sailors welcome it and call it Saint Elmo's Fire. Their guardian is protecting the ship.'

Kerta looked at him and began to smile. 'Like a wizard. Saint Elmo is stopping Antoe Laoet and Orang Aljeh from attacking the *Loudon*.'

'I guess so.'

Schruit tapped his ribbon. 'Well, that lot will be in Batavia in an hour. The line will be back any minute.'

'Maybe Harbourmaster van Leewen is right, it is only a toothless tiger.' Lloyd's Agent Schuit passed a slice of ginger cake to Kerta.

Kerta looked at the comfortable men and he began feeling a little better. There *is* a wizard for the boats . . . He looked over the bridge's rail to the canal's other side where the boats were more protected. There was a *proa* drifting, another *proa*'s sail was half in the water, *Goliath* was covered with sodden ash, but there were no boats sunk. And Lloyd's Agent Schuit would repair and clean his *Goliath* today. And Master Telegrapher Schruit would send his tiny lightning sparks around the world in less than an hour.

He turned back to the other side of the canal as he bit into his ginger cake.

The canal is all right. They can fix the drawbridge, but why fix it anyway? It's something that goes with the fort, and that is abandoned. The people in the beach kampong can use this bridge. And the *proas* can be repaired – all of them. Even the schooner . . .

Kerta frowned as his eyes caught movement through the ship's rigging. Something like a brown fog on the water. Moving fast. 'Ah, Tuan Schruit –'

'Jesus Christ!'

sea wave

KERTA could not understand what he was seeing. Out there in Sunda Strait was a grey wall that blocked the entire horizon from Krakatoa to Thwart-the-Way Island. It was moving towards the canal.

A great wall of water was scudding over the sea at him. It was beginning to roar, coming faster than a clipper ship, and it was high. Higher than that schooner's mainmast. The wall of water was twelve metres high. And there were two more behind it.

Kerta was gaping, thinking that it couldn't be, until Schruit punched him hard on the shoulder and shouted, 'Run like hell!'

But as Schruit shouted he ran *towards* the wall of water!

Kerta leaped from the rail as Lloyd's Agent Schuit jumped into the canal.

Schruit shrieked at the linemen, 'Get out, get out, run! Sea wave!' Only then he began to gallop away.

Kerta sprinted across the bridge as the roar grew louder, *proas* splintering behind him. He skidded off the bridge, turned into a short lane in the Arab Quarter, and saw an old man peering at him from a shop. As he shot past the shop he yelled at him, 'Run!' For a second he was running along the canal and could see both Schruit and Schuit.

Schuit had not dropped into the water when he leaped from the bridge, but onto a *proa*, and now he was clambering across other boats towards *Goliath*. Schruit was darting around bushes on the other side of the canal, further back than Schuit.

They won't make it, Kerta thought.

The roar was getting closer and now there were terrible screams inside the roar.

Schruit won't make it, Schuit won't make it.

Nobody will make it.

Kerta sucked air into his aching lungs and realised that he couldn't keep on sprinting like he was. There will be a tree, or rice paddy, or he will run out of steam and that monster sea wave will swallow him. His eyes began to stretch wide as he ran.

I am going to die . . .

The canal crashed and thudded beside him. *Proas* surged through the canal, thumping at each other and the wooden walls. In the middle of the chaos there was *Goliath* with Lloyd's Agent Schuit grimly riding it.

Kerta could feel the shaking of the ground as he veered away from the canal. He told himself not to look back.

But the roar was biting his ears, so he looked. And the wall of water was less than three metres behind him, like a tiger springing.

The only thing he could do was leap at the trunk of a coconut tree. And hang on.

He locked his arms, legs, around the tree, took a very short breath and closed his eyes. Then the wave hit.

The water clutched Kerta and shook his body like a dog with a rag. It thundered past his ears, pushed into his nostrils, jerked his head about, battered his back, and pulled at his legs. He felt the coconut tree leaning, his arms and legs slipping along the trunk. He tried to increase his grip, but his left leg was whipped from the trunk and he couldn't bring it back against the incredible power of the wave. All he could do was push his head hard against the tree, squeeze his eyelids and hold on to what he still had.

After a long time his eyelids lightened and the pressure dropped. He was able to pull his leg back to the trunk and the tree started to lift.

He thought, Maybe I can breathe . . .

But then the next wave hit, darkening his eyelids again, and scraping him along the trunk until his feet touched the fronds.

He thought, The tree has been ripped out of the ground!

But when the second wave passed, the trunk began to rise again.

He thought, Air, air . . .

And he spun on the trunk like a monkey before the third wave. A frond slapped his face. His eyelids became lighter and he opened his eyes, pleading for a view above water. But he saw rushing brown water.

His lungs strained at the lock he had clamped over his throat, tearing it apart.

Can't hold it, can't hold –

He gasped.

Air flooded into his lungs, he shook his head and a brief stream from a frond poured into his ear. He looked down as the third wave rushed under him and the coconut tree lifted back. He coughed and panted heavily as he wiped his eyes with the back of his arm; then he looked.

'Oh, Allah . . .'

Anjer was gone. From his swaying coconut tree to the mists of the strait was a vast, seething sea. There was no sign of the canal, only the schooner rushing after the wreckage of what had been many *proas*. The schooner had a terrible list and the foremast was dragging beside the hull. The wharves had disappeared and between that whirling water and the canal where was nothing but flattened and shattered trees. The bunkhouses of the fort were gone, the singing mosque, the bridge, the Arab lane he had run through minutes ago, the market, the Chinese Quarter, the Waterfront – Li Yang's shop, Baha's shop, Captain De Jong's ship chandler and the Schuits' hotel – all gone. The Master Telegrapher's office, gone, the church, gone, the great house of the Assistant Resident, gone, except for the tall flagstaff with the flag still drifting in the air.

In a few minutes Anjer had ceased to exist.

survivors

KERTA could hear his pulse thundering in his ears and he shook his head to clear out the water. Immediately he wanted to slap his hands over his ears to block out the sounds. Water was roaring past his coconut tree, sluicing around the trunk as he felt its force with his fingers. Bits of wood were thudding, scraping, being pulled apart and snapping. Stones were tumbling, crashing into metal. But much worse were the cries of people, from far away, from very close, and sometimes he thought he heard a small girl calling. And then he heard someone crying out faintly, directly below him. He looked down and saw a Chinese old man – he might have been the man Kerta had shouted to in the lane – clinging to his tree. He was looking up at Kerta and reaching towards him with a quivering hand as the foaming water surged around his head.

'I –' Kerta moved, but then felt the tree dip and he tightened his grip.

The old man's hand sagged, dropped to the trunk, but his eyes were still locked on Kerta's.

Kerta stared back as he slowly shook his head.

The water heaved around the old man's head, slinging his pigtail across his face and the foam began to cover his eyes.

Kerta shook his head and climbed come down, squeezing his legs and hands on the rough trunk, until he was close to the roaring water and the old man. 'Hey!' He reached down with his right hand, but the old man's face was now below the surface. Kerta stretched beyond his locked feet, to the water and touched the old man's hand.

The old man lifted his head and his hand groped in the air for a moment, but then his body was turned by the current. He was jerked from the tree and carried away. Kerta watched him until he disappeared.

He thought, I will go soon too.

There was another crack from Krakatoa.

Kerta slinked back to the top of the tree and after a while there were no more cries.

* * *

He hung onto the fronds for a while, and then he noticed a different sound coming from the water. When he looked he saw the water beginning to flow back to the sea. He felt the tree tremble, and he clung as he saw wreckage race past. The schooner lurched through the trees near him, stopped and tilted. Suddenly he could see the hotel floating out of the jungle as if it was a riverboat. For one moment he thought that the hotel had survived the waves and was returning to its old place, but then it snagged a corner and Kerta slowly saw as it turned that there was no side to the hotel, no back, no roof. It was like a painting from Joost's house, but then that changed too as the last wall crumbled into the rushing water.

The lighthouse, he thought dully. That has gone too. Ma has gone. And Pa, Dewi.

Kerta sagged in the fronds and brought the back of his arm to his face.

No! He shook his head. Fourth Point is not a rickety wooden hotel or a sinking schooner, it is granite and iron and it's tall. It *can* beat those sea waves!

He pulled his arm back, almost angrily.

But . . .

He screwed his eyes shut. Shut up, shut up, shut up. You've got to get home, now!

He stared at the rushing water under the tree, felt the trunk shaking, heard the clashing of wood and metal, and did not move.

*   *   *

Finally he fell from the tree, splashing into the muddy water. He threw his arms around in confusion until his feet found the ground, and staggered to his feet. He didn't know whether he had gone to sleep in the fronds or the tree had shrugged him out, but it didn't matter now. He was down, and the water only waist deep. Now he could get home.

But when he began to wade through the water he felt a throbbing ache. He looked at his right arm and immediately pain shot through his arms and legs. In his battle with the surging water he had been scraped against the rough trunk and his skin was scored with deep scratches and gashes. His shirt was torn and hanging from his shoulders like rags. His sandals had been ripped from his feet.

But none of these things really mattered.

He bent over to put his arms into the muddy water to cool them a little and then began to wade slowly towards home. It was a very hard journey – for a start, he didn't know where he was. He knew that the coast was on his right hand because the water was rushing to it, and there was a misty jungle on his left, but that was almost everything. He was wading across a wasteland with rubble and ripped-out trees, without a single recognisable point.

A tangle of wreckage charged towards him and he had to throw himself into the water to avoid it. He struggled for a while in the current, spinning, floundering, until his foot snagged a root.

A man on a branch waved as he floated past and Kerta tried to hurry after him, until he realised that the branch was moving the man's arm. The man was dead. Kerta turned away and saw three more bodies, two women and a small boy, floating past him. He tried to keep moving without looking at the water, but he couldn't. The only thing he could do was blank out his mind. He would register a tree, floating timber, rubble and that was all.

Until he heard a call for him.

He stopped in the water and he wasn't quite sure his ears had actually caught his name.

'Kerta!' It was faint but desperate.

He slowly turned his head, and saw Jan on a small pile of rubble fifty metres away.

He thought, No, I can't help; I've got to go home.

But he sloshed towards Jan.

Jan's left leg was trapped by a heavy stone lintel and his face was strained with pain. 'What happened?' Jan was slurring.

Kerta shook his head. 'A wave, many of them, I don't know.' He grabbed the stone and heaved.

Jan screamed.

Kerta jerked his hands from the stone. 'Sorry, sorry.'

Jan closed his eyes. 'It's all right.'

Kerta looked around for help.

'There's nobody left. Papa and Mama gone. I saw that . . .'

Kerta turned to him, but he didn't know what to say.

A heavy stone splashed into the water near them. They watched fragments of skeletons bobbing in the rushing flood as another tombstone gave way. Jan was pinned in the rubble of the church and its cemetery was giving up its dead.

'Will it come again?' Jan said quietly.

Kerta stared at Jan. 'I – we have to try again.'

'Yes.' Jan nodded once.

Kerta grabbed the stone as Jan jammed his hands in the

rubble. 'All right?' Then Kerta bared his teeth at Jan and heaved at the stone. Jan screamed at him, Kerta shrieked at him and kept on heaving until Jan fell backwards. Kerta helped him from the water but Jan couldn't put his left foot down.

'Is it bad?' Kerta said, looking in the direction of home.

'Yeah,' Jan said thickly. He lifted his foot from the water, and the bone of his ankle was poking through his skin.

Kerta winced. He opened his mouth, then shook his head and closed it. He put Jan's arm across his neck and they staggered from the rubble of the church towards the jungle. As they lurched away from the ruins of Anjer the water dropped away, but large pieces of pumice began to rain upon them. They tried to protect their heads in a huddle as they moved, but it wasn't working and the air was thick with ash. Jan was staggering against Kerta, gasping for each step as if he was trying to fall into the water. Finally Kerta saw a large log. He dumped Jan and staggered a step away.

'We'll just have a bit of a rest,' Kerta panted and held his side.

Jan stared at the water between his knees and wheezed heavily. Then he looked up at Kerta and blinked at him as if he had not seen him until now. 'You . . .' He gasped and waved him away.

Kerta stepped back uncertainty.

'You . . . have not seen your . . . family.' Jan was beginning to control his breathing.

Kerta said nothing.

'Before you were going back to the lighthouse.'

'Yes.'

'You leave now. I will rest here, I'll be right.'

Kerta hesitated, and then nodded. 'Yes, I have to.' He tried to make a half-smile at Jan and sloshed away from him. After ten metres he looked back.

Jan waved him away, almost in annoyance. 'Go on; go on, I'll be all right. You'll find them, you'll see.'

Kerta turned again and moved towards the river. Shortly in the fog of the ash and the falling pumice he saw a shadow lurching towards the jungle. 'Hey, hey.'

The shadow stopped and peered at him. 'Kerta?'

'Dungu?' Kerta hurried and then slowed down.

The fisherman's face had been gashed on the left side and his eyes were looking through Kerta. His clothes were sodden, torn, and blood dripped from the gash onto his shirt. His right hand wandered to the trees behind him. 'It's gone now; nothing at all.'

Kerta stared at him. 'The lighthouse?'

'The kampong, the *proas*, huts, the goats, the wife, everyone . . .'

'The lighthouse! Is that gone too?'

'Lighthouse . . .' Dungu frowned slowly. 'I don't know.'

'You didn't see how it looked?'

'I was looking for my wife . . . Who's that?'

Kerta looked back and saw Jan hunched with his hands covering his eyes. 'Oh. The Dutch boy on *Goliath*. With the net.'

'Your friend.'

Kerta blinked and slowly nodded. 'Yes, my friend. He has lost his parents . . .'

'Oh. And you're going away.' Dungu looked into his eyes. 'Yes, of course. You won't be able to use the road bridge but the waterworks' rope bridge is still there. I crossed it. I'll stay with the Dutch boy. We share something.'

Kerta watched the sad fisherman lurch towards Jan and then moved away with a sick feeling. He found the waterworks by recognising two *warignen* trees on the other side of the river. The rope bridge was dipping into the river, catching branches and fragments of huts, and it would collapse in a few minutes. He clambered quickly onto the bridge as the ropes creaked frighteningly. He climbed the top rope to get over the dip and saw a vague white shape below the surface of the river and it might have been a body. His eyes lifted from the water as he pulled himself to the other side.

There was a sharp crack behind him as he moved through the flooded trees, but he didn't look back. Almost immediately Krakatoa exploded again. Kerta shook his head as if he had been hit and tottered a little. That was the fourth incredible explosion from Krakatoa in four hours.

What is happening there? he thought.

He began to wade out of the trees, but he slowed down as he looked around.

It doesn't matter now, he thought. Krakatoa, Orang Aljeh and Antoe Laoet have destroyed everything. There is nothing left for them.

He knew where he was, but it had changed forever. His feet were finding the roots of rice from the spreading paddies and he should be seeing the clustered huts of the kampong and the *proa* beach, but he was surrounded by a silent lake. The lake stretched to the edges of the jungle and the lapping sea.

Kerta felt that he was the only person in the world.

But then he saw a yellow glimmer in the dark sky. He stared at it and slowly picked out a white column from the yellow light down to the trees.

The Fourth Point was still standing!

Kerta squelched across the lake, through tangled trees, past some wreckage to the wooden bridge. The Great Post Road was still underwater but he could cross the river by balancing himself across the rail. He splashed towards the towering lighthouse and then his charge petered out.

I knew it, he thought. I knew it . . .

the lighthouse

THE path to the lighthouse was a cataract. The water eddied past trapped thatching and broken timber on both sides of the lighthouse. The large water tank had disappeared without the slightest sign and Jacob's bungalow was nothing but a stick leaning on a tree. The flagpole had been snapped like a twig. The Brothers' and Carver's huts were gone.

And the hut where Kerta, Pa, Ma and Dewi slept, ate and lived had vanished. As if the family had never existed.

Kerta stumbled towards where the hut used to be as his throat thickened. 'Ah, Allah . . .'

'Kerta!'

He swivelled in the flowing water and saw a small figure in the light of the open door of the lighthouse. 'Dewi?' He tried to run through the water.

The little girl turned around and yelled into the lighthouse and then splashed towards him.

Ma darted into the light and cried, 'Praise Allah!' She rushed to him.

The three bodies clashed together in the water, with

arms clinging on like chains, and then Ma pushed Dewi and Kerta towards the open door. They mumbled to each other as they shuffled together without really understanding what they were saying. It was enough just to hear the sound of each other's voices.

But when Kerta stepped into the glow of the lantern in the lighthouse Ma stared at him in horror. 'What happened to you?'

'Where's Pa?'

'He's all right – he's up the top. Fighting his battle. You'll have to go up there to show that you've come back. But not yet. Dewi, get me some water and salt.'

'Salt?' Kerta frowned.

Ma started to pull his ragged shirt off his back. 'You're covered in leeches.'

He looked down and saw the fat black slugs on his chest and legs, especially where the skin was raw, and shivered. 'Bloody things.'

'And these?' She touched a red scrape.

'The sea wave tried to pull me from a coconut tree.'

'We knew it was very bad in Anjer . . .'

'It's gone, everything, and the kampong.'

'Everything?'

'I saw bodies floating past –'

Ma lifted her hand as Dewi brought the bowl of salt. 'The Brothers, Carver and Rara had the right idea, I think. When we came home yesterday afternoon they were gone. Pa thought they had gone into the hills.'

'I think I saw Carver and Rara going through the market last night.'

'Ah well . . .'

'I told everybody that you would come back.' Dewi nodded furiously at him. 'Didn't I, Ma?'

Kerta saw that her face was streaked with tears.

'Yes, you were right. Smarter than a tree of monkeys.' Ma dipped her fingers into the salt and rubbed lightly onto Kerta's leeches. The leeches coiled and dropped from him. 'We should have taken the hint from the Brothers, Carver and Rara,' she said to Kerta.

Dewi screwed up her nose. 'Do they hurt?'

'No. They just look awful.'

'But we are the Lighthouse Keeper's family, so we are here.' Ma suddenly laughed brittly. 'And of course, we had to wait.'

'Sorry. I should have come before.'

Ma shook her head as she turned him around. 'It wouldn't have made any difference. If I had wanted to go into the hills, maybe if you were here I could have persuaded Pa to leave the lighthouse. There was Dewi after all. Maybe. But there was Jacob. The Master Lighthouse Keeper would not leave his lighthouse and that was that. If Jacob is staying then Pa, the Lighthouse Keeper, is also staying.'

'Jacob is still here, then?' Kerta felt her tightening her hand on his arm.

'No.'

'The big waves,' Dewi said quietly.

Ma turned sharply. 'I didn't know you had seen it.'

'I heard the sound.'

Ma grabbed and pressed Dewi to her body. 'Shush, shush.'

'The house fell.'

'Yes, yes. It was terrible. But maybe Jacob and his twins are in the jungle safe. They may have climbed a tree like Kerta . . .'

Dewi looked at Kerta and then shook her head. 'No.'

Ma slowly nodded. 'Smarter than a tree of monkeys.' She looked up to Kerta. 'Jacob had been listening to the Harbourmaster say that Krakatoa had finished and he'd gone to bed in his bungalow with the twins. No matter what Pa said to him . . .'

She pushed Dewi back and looked into her eyes. 'It was terrible, really terrible. But remember, Pa saved us. He took us out of our hut, put us here, surrounded by thick stone. Look at it.' She reached back and pounded the granite wall. 'Jacob should have listened to Pa.'

Dewi peered over Ma's shoulder at the wall. 'It was so big and loud. I felt the wall shaking. What if it is coming back?'

'It won't, but we have the lighthouse. The mighty lighthouse.'

Dewi shook her head. 'It won't because Pa is up there making the volcano stop.'

Ma nodded tiredly. 'Must be.' She turned to Kerta. 'You better go up to see Pa, show that you're here.'

Kerta wobbled fingers at Dewi and began to climb the lighthouse.

He was about halfway up when he slapped his hands against his ears, threw his mouth wide open and stumbled backward on the iron steps. There had been a shattering explosion, so massive that the granite wall of the Fourth Point was quivering. For a second he thought the lighthouse was collapsing and he knew that it was from Krakatoa and he knew this time was far greater than all the others. He leaned against one of the girders and tried to listen through the singing in his ears. He thought he would hear that singing sound for ever.

He realised that he had heard the other four explosions in the open air, but this sound had blasted through the thick granite wall of the lighthouse. Surely his eardrums would have burst if he had been a little closer to Krakatoa. But after a while he began to hear a faint sound over the singing.

Dewi was screaming.

Kerta started to hurry back, and then she slowly quietened. He thought, Ma is holding her now. There is nothing you can do.

He turned around and climbed to the lantern room. Pa was leaning into the machinery as if he had not heard the sound.

'Pa?' Kerta called from the steps, but Pa kept on working with the lantern clockwork. 'Pa . . .' Kerta stepped into the room and shouted.

Pa turned with a vague frown, and then he saw Kerta.

He pulled a screwdriver from the machinery, sagged to the floor and made a weak smile at him. 'You're here.'

Kerta shrugged.

Pa scrabbled across the floor like a spider. He sprang to his feet and crushed Kerta to him. 'We thought . . .' He shook his head.

'Dewi didn't.'

'No, she didn't. Must have been bad.'

'Dewi was screaming with the last boom.'

'Ma is there.'

'Ma wants to leave the lighthouse.'

Pa shook his head. 'I cannot.'

'Because you're fighting with ghosts . . .'

Pa stepped back, looked at Kerta and rushed him up the stairs and out into the gallery. 'Look now, boy!'

Kerta blinked in the powerful beam and saw a red glow in the sky above Krakatoa. 'I see the Orang Aljeh.' He thought, It is answering Fourth Point . . .

'There is more. Jacob – my friend – died with his twins at the hands of Orang Aljeh and Antoe Laoet, but do you think he would have stayed here to fight ghosts? *That* is what he stayed for.' Pa pointed at a feeble green light bobbing between Krakatoa and the lighthouse. 'And that.' He swung his finger to a tiny glimmer of white.

'Ships,' Kerta said dully.

'The first one I don't know, it's sailing ship, it doesn't matter. The other one, I think is the *Loudon*.'

Kerta's face lightened. 'There?' He squinted at the

pinpoint of light. 'Their wizard has beaten them . . .' And then the light disappeared.

'I can't do anything for the kampong or Anjer, but I can help those sailors now. Maybe later the light attracted help.'

The green light vanished.

Pa started to move back. 'Jacob would like that.'

'Pa . . .'

Pa half-smiled. 'But, yes, I guess this light is also for the ghosts. It's for Jacob and for Orang Aljeh and Antoe Laoet. Tell the ghosts we are still here!' He punched the air.

'Pa, there's something out there!'

The fist dropped away. 'I – Get down there!' Pa snatched Kerta from the gallery and hurled him down the ladder.

Kerta stumbled on the rungs, his eyes wide, staring and blind.

'No!' Pa's foot caught on the ladder. He was looking *back* – away from the sea.

Then Kerta was away from the ladder, the clicking of the lantern machinery, the ticking of the clock, 10.45, and down the steps, past the red girders. The thunder of Pa's feet behind him, then nothing. Something dropped past him and then Pa was wobbling on the floor below, and down the next flight.

Pa is panicking, shimmered across Kerta's mind.

He could see the terrible image still in his eyes as the twisting steps flicked past, the red girders, the granite wall . . . He had seen all the dark water of Sunda Strait rearing far above the top of the lighthouse.

*　　*　　*

It was as if the world had jerked to a stop and all the oceans had whipped from their muddy beds. The Doomsday story he had told Dewi was happening.

He ran and jumped down the lighthouse with a slither of thought: If there was any hope to survive this, it would be in the base of the Fourth Point. Where Ma and Dewi are, where Pa is racing to, where *he* was trying to reach before the ocean fell.

But then he looked through one of the lighthouse long windows as he raced and he began to understand why Pa had charged down. As he had been running, he had held the image in his mind; there was brightness on the ground where the keepers' huts had been and that light shouldn't be there. There was a small shadow jerking away from the lighthouse . . .

He stopped thinking about that as he skidded down the last flight. He saw that the lighthouse door was open wide.

'Ma!' He shouted as he ran to the door.

The ground under his feet was shaking; a great thunderous roar swept over his ears.

Everything had slowed. Pa, Ma and Dewi were wooden carvings on the wet path. Pa's foot was splashing into a muddy puddle, his mouth gaping wide as an arm reached desperately towards Ma. But the distance was too far. Ma was twenty metres away from him. She had raced desperately after Dewi and Pa must have seen Dewi running. Now Ma was snatching Dewi from the shallow water as she looked back at Pa. Dewi's legs were dancing in the air, mouth open and eyes staring up into the sky . . .

Kerta looked up. To the high white tower of the Fourth Point, to the lantern, to its black hat, to the massive grey wave looming over it. The wave crashed against the lantern, the tower, and grey fingers clutched around the base. He stumbled back and heard a mighty crash on the other side of the lighthouse, and then he saw the granite blocks lurching apart, the red girders folding and screaming . . .

the light

A LONELY hoot pulled Kerta from his blackness. His eyes blinked open. He could hear running water, the creaking of iron and a steady throbbing beat near by. After another blast from the whistle he peered between some granite blocks to see a ship moving slowly at the edge of the shallow water.

The ship was the *Loudon*, but it had changed. It was covered in black ash, from derricks, booms, rails, the glass windows on the bridge to all of the decks. The ash on the bridge and the funnel was glinting with salt. It looked like it had come from the bottom of the sea and any moment the engine would shiver it back down. He could see Captain Lindemann staring at the lighthouse from the bridge wing and a few men were leaning on the deck railing. For a moment Kerta thought he could see Hasan among them.

The steam whistle blasted again and he tried to get up, but he felt the shock of pain in his right leg and fell back. He shouted and waved, but the whistle stopped as *Loudon* slid away.

His head sagged to the sodden wood. He attempted to

pull his leg to him, but a hot knife shot through his body. Gritting his teeth, he turned and saw a massive pile of rubble and girders on his leg. The Fourth Point was no more than a broken rim of stone and warped iron.

Then Kerta remembered what he had seen and he fell back, as if trying to escape from the memory. His trapped leg slid from the rubble. For a few moments he looked stupidly at the slow-bleeding leg, then dragged himself to his feet. He climbed out of the wreckage and looked out.

The *Loudon* was gone now. There was a great lump of coral jammed against the wreckage of the lighthouse. The trees were a stack of driftwood. The coconut trees had been ripped from the ground and thrown against the heavy jungle trees, where branches had been torn from the trunks. Any branches still clinging to the trees had been stripped of leaves. There were no signs of Ma, Pa, Dewi . . .

He limped away from the lighthouse and watched the carcass of a water buffalo drifting with the tide. A horn dipped and nodded, giving the buffalo a fake touch of life.

Kerta thought very slowly, There is nobody left now.

Jacob Schuit, Master Lighthouse Keeper, Adam and Dirck. The Imam was singing at the mosque when the first wave came, Li Yang would have have opening his shop at the same time. Lloyd's Agent Schuit, Kerta had last seen riding the edge of the wave on *Goliath*, Master Telegrapher Schruit racing through the trees with the water gnawing at his heels.

Gone, gone.

245

My friends, Bas and Jan. Gone . . .

But maybe Ma, Pa, Dewi beat it. Maybe . . .

His eye caught a small piece of brown cloth snagged on a branch. There was something about it that tickled his memory, and he moved closer. He swallowed thickly, reached for the brown cloth, pulled it from the tangled leaves and looked at the sodden lump in his hand.

Then he remembered his last glimpse of them. He had turned from the wall of water. Motionless like a statue, but Pa had seemed to look at him as the Fourth Point crashed around them and the huge wave coiled down. And then nothing.

Very slowly he then sagged into a pool of water, as if his legs were straw.

'Why?' He mumbled softly.

He held a torn doll. The drawn eyes stared at him, the crooked mouth made a sad grimace in the light cream head. It was a Dutch doll, but Dewi had made it hers.

'Why?' He slowly lifted his head and saw the ruined lighthouse, a pile of stone with girders thrusting out of it. A pinnacle of granite remained, like a tombstone.

Kerta pulled himself from the muddy water and lurched back to the ruin with the doll in his hand. He slowly hunted around the rubble, finding rope, two kerosene tins, and three lanterns. He even found a prism of glass from the lens in the lighthouse lantern. He managed to snap a cracked water pipe and began to lash the prism and three lanterns to the pipe.

He filled the lanterns with the kerosene, lit them, lifted the water pipe beyond the pinnacle and lashed it to a girder. The light from the lanterns threw a glow over the ruin and out across the Sunda Strait.

Kerta thrust his fist at the smoking carcass of Krakatoa. 'We are still here!'

epilogue

On Thursday, 10 May 1883, a massive rock plate nudged a greater plate under Krakatoa. The Australian tectonic plate – carrying Australia, New Zealand and part of the Indian, Southern and Pacific oceans – had been sliding slowly across the liquid magma against the Eurasian plate for thousands of years. This movement had caused hundreds of earthquakes and volcanic eruptions in Indonesia, but the pressure point of these two plates is Krakatoa. When the eruption occurred it was like the mighty crash of an articulated lorry with a freight train, but very, very, slow. The Australian plate had been moving under the Eurasian plate – the subduction zone – and pressed the liquid magma. There were at least two great eruptions at Krakatoa before, once in prehistory and once about 530 AD. On 10 May 1883, there were only a few vibrations, but it was the beginning.

Ten days later the Australian plate pushed at a magma chamber under Krakatoa, forcing steam and ash through one of Krakatoa's craters – Perboewatan. After a while the volcano subsided, but in June the Australian plate was moving again. Black smoke, new vents between Perboewatan and Danan, violent eruptions and strange tides showed that Krakatoa was building up.

On Sunday August 26 at 1.06 pm a rumble marked the beginning of the final stage. Ships passing Krakatoa saw a black cloud of ash rising as high as 27 kilometres, and their decks were covered by a heavy ash fall, with pieces of large hot pumice. The shaking of the volcano caused freak waves and a small tsunami.

There were ships trapped by the waves in Kampong Bay that night, including the Dutch gunship *Berouw* and *Gouverneur-Generaal Loudon*. *Berouw* was anchored near the jetty of Telok Betong, forced to stay there because her paddles could not deal with the waves. The only thing the crew could do was throw more anchors and hope. Captain Lindemann could not tie *Loudon* up to the jetty at Telok Betong so he had to drop an anchor in the middle of Kampong Bay with his passengers, convicts and the Chinese workers. The wind was coming straight from Krakatoa, bringing thick ash, pumice and mud rain. In the thunderstorm *Loudon* was struck by lightning many times, with Saint Elmo's fire phosphorescent on the masts, rigging and decks.

On August 27 at 5.30 am there was a deafening explosion at Krakatoa as the island began to sink and water hit the white-hot magma. From that, tsunamis rushed from Krakatoa and ripped *Berouw* from her anchors and threw her to the Chinese quarter in Telok Betong. Across the Sunda Strait, Pilot de Vries was walking along the beach when he saw the first tsunami. He ran into Anjer shouting, and survived. Master Telegrapher Schruit ran for three kilometres to a safe village. Lloyd's Agent Schuit rode the tsunami on a boat, but he lost his family.

At 10.02 am there was the final explosion, the worst. It was even heard in Perth, Australia, 3,500 kilometres away, and the island of Rodriguez near Madagascar, 4,800 kilometres away. The eruptions had pulled from the Earth 21 cubic kilometres of rock fragments, and dust particles reached high into the atmosphere, eventually spreading round the world. Dramatic sunsets were seen in London, New York, Sydney, all over the world – and the blood-red sky of Edvard Munch's famous 1893 painting *The Scream* showed the sky over Norway after the eruption. The dust cooled the Earth's temperature by 1.2 degrees Celcius for about five years.

Perboewatan, 122 metres high, Danan, 445 metres and most of Rakata, 823 metres, had disappeared. Where there had been a sheer cliff in the remains of Rakata there was a hole, a caldera, 250 metres deep. On that morning Krakatoa dropped into the empty space.

The massive slump left the highly pressurised magma chamber wide open to the sea and that was what caused the boom – the loudest sound ever recorded, concussive air waves that travelled seven times around the world – and the tsunamis. Some of them eventually hit Hawaii, South Africa and were even noticed in the English Channel. In the Sunda Strait they were up to a height of forty metres.

Captain Lindemann saw that monster from the bridge of *Loudon*, but the only thing he could do was steer at it. The

Loudon burrowed into the wave for a long time, but then she began to rise. She had survived, but the wave was racing to Telok Betong. It picked up *Berouw* from the ruined Chinese Quarter and dumped it three kilometres up the Kuripan River.

Another tsunami surged under the barque *Charles Bal* and hit the Fourth Point Lighthouse, along with a massive lump of coral, destroying it.

After the tsunamis a hot cloud of ash – pyroclastic flows – raced from Krakatoa to Kampong Bay. The ash hit Willem Beyerinck's family, high above Kalimbang, killing his baby and many Sumatrans around his family. The tsunamis and the pyroclastic flows combined to destroy 165 villages and towns and kill more than 36,400 people in Sumatra and Java.

Captain Lindemann took *Loudon* close to the ruin of Fourth Point, a stump, but could not see any life. He dropped anchor at Anjer and went ashore to see if he could help. There was nothing to do but pick up a few survivors. He sailed to Batavia.

Now Anjer has become Anyer, a tourist beach resort, and Fourth Point has gone, apart from the brick and concrete foundation of the lighthouse and the water tank. There is a newer lighthouse fifty metres inland from the foundation.

Krakatoa is coming back. In 1927 Anak Krakatau (Child of Krakatau) appeared where Perboewatan had been and has been growing solidly ever since.

But when Captain Lindemann sailed past the ruin of Fourth Point it had not finished. One of the Javanese lighthouse keepers had lost his wife and boy, but went back to the wreckage and within six hours he had given Fourth Point a light.

We don't know his name.

author's note

This book could not have been written without:

Krakatoa, the Day World Exploded: August 27, 1883, Simon Winchester, Perennial, New York, US, 2003

Krakatoa, Rupert Funeaux, Prentice-Hall, Englewood Cliffs, US, 1964

The Conquest of Java – Nineteenth-century Java seen through the eyes of a soldier of the British Empire, Major William Thorn, Periplus Editions, Singapore, 2004

Catastrophe, an Investigation into the Origins of the Modern World, David Keys, Ballantine Books, New York, US, 1999.

1883	Now
Anjer	Anyer
Batavia	Jakarta
Dutch East Indies	Indonesia
Fourth Point	Cikoneng
Krakatoa	Anak Krakatoa
Pepper Bay	Teluk Lada
Telok Betong	Bandar Lampung
Thwart-the-Way	Sangiang

about the author

Allan Baillie was born in Scotland in 1943 and came to Victoria, Australia with his family when he was six. They moved to Emerald, then Geelong (he still barracks for the Cats), Drysdale, Portarlington and later Melbourne.

Allan began writing stories for fun while still at school. He is now one of Australia's most successful writers for children. His novels, which include *Little Brother* (1986), *The China Coin* (1992), *Saving Abbie* (2000) and *Treasure Hunters* (2002), have won him acclaim, awards and international recognition. His books have found success in Japan, Sweden, Holland, Germany, France, Spain, the United Kingdom, the United States, New Zealand and South Africa. His most recent books for Penguin include a collection of short stories, *A Taste of Cockroach* (2005) and *Castles* (2005), a superb picture book for young children, illustrated by Caroline Magerl.

Allan spends most of his time with his wife Agnes in Avalon, north of Sydney, but they travel regularly to far-flung places, including Anak Krakatoa, the Son of Krakatoa, which they climbed during a quiet period.

You can find out more about Allan Baillie at allanbaillie.com.au.

ABOVE *Allan Baillie with his wife Agnes on Anak Krakatoa*

If you're a reader who likes
to win prizes, hear from your
favourite authors and find out
about new books before
anybody else . . .

Then you need to subscribe to
SQUAWK – an e-mail newsletter
with all the latest on books
from Penguin for readers
who are aged 8-13.

Just visit
puffin.com.au
and click on the link to

THE

SQUAWK